# Seven Islands of the Ocmulgee

Gordon Johnston's *Seven Islands of the Ocmulgee* is not a quiet book of meditations on a river. Rather, it is a deeply engaging set of intertwined stories that feature the complexity of character one associates with literary fiction while also offering surprising, twisty plots that send the reader rocketing through the pages. This is a terrific book. I loved reading it.

> —Robert Boswell, author of *Tumbledown, Mystery Ride,*
> *Century's Son,* and *The Heyday of the Insensitive Bastards*

Gordon Johnston writes these stories in sharp, terse sentences about the river he knows so well. With a knack for dialogue, he creates characters from the inside-out, making them absolutely real to the reader. We find ourselves in the minds of Rea, tense as she maneuvers her kayak through a difficult stretch of rapids, frantic to save a boy on the shore, and a stranger "whose beard flowed black with river..." Deep revelation into the minds and hearts of these Southerners combined fast-paced adventure makes *Seven Islands of the Ocmulgee* a delightful read.

> —Melanie Sumner, author of *How to Write a Novel: A Novel*

The river that runs through this book is made of Gordon Johnston's fine, musical prose, and the stories he tells are at once ancient and modern, as humans from our busy, self-satisfied world intersect with aspects of the past that haunt us still. In "The Only Place to Start From," a First Nations youth recruits a Publix grocery store manager to help him on the start of a life journey; in "Burying Ground" members of a church travel through a mill village to find an old riverside for a baptism and encounter a battle with old sins as they do. Each story is finely wrought, complex, worth pondering for a goodly while. A reader can't ask for more. This is a fine book by one of Georgia's best writers.

> —Jim Grimsley, author of *Winter Birds,*
> *Dream Boy,* and *The Dove in the Belly*

*Also by Gordon Johnston*

*Ocmulgee National Monument: A Brief Guide with Field Notes* (with Matthew Jennings; 2017)

*The Things of Earth* (poetry chapbook; 2007)

*Scaring the Bears: Poems* (2021)
Winner of the 2022 Lilly Fellows Program Arlin G. Meyer Prize in Imaginative Writing

*Durable Goods* (poetry chapbook; 2021)

*Where Here Is Hard to Say: Poems* (forthcoming)

# Seven Islands of the Ocmulgee

[River Stories]

## Gordon Johnston

MERCER UNIVERSITY PRESS
*Macon, Georgia*
*with*
GEORGIA HUMANITIES

MUP/ P666

© 2023 by Mercer University Press
Published by Mercer University Press
1501 Mercer University Drive
Macon, Georgia 31207

27  26  25  24  23       5  4  3  2  1

Books published by Mercer University Press are printed on acid-free paper that meets the requirements of the American National Standard for Information Sciences—Permanence of Paper for Printed Library Materials.

Printed and bound in the United States.
This book is set in Adobe Caslon Pro and Georgia (display).
Cover/jacket design by Burt&Burt.

Library of Congress Cataloging-in-Publication Data
Names: Johnston, Gordon, 1967- author.
Title: Seven islands of the Ocmulgee : river stories / Gordon Johnston.
Identifiers: LCCN 2022044898 | ISBN 9780881468793 (paperback) |
      ISBN   9780881468809 (ebook)
Subjects: LCSH: Ocmulgee River (Ga.)—Fiction. | LCGFT: Short
      stories.
Classification: LCC PS3610.O386 S48 2023 | DDC 813/.6—
      dc23/eng/20221021
LC record available at https://lccn.loc.gov/2022044898

*In memory of*

*Jane Snead Cofer, Wilson Hall, and Jim Kilgo*

**50**

**Georgia Humanities**

Celebrating 50 years of sharing stories
that move us and make us

# Contents

MERCER UNIVERSITY PRESS

*Endowed by*

TOM WATSON BROWN
*and*
THE WATSON-BROWN FOUNDATION, INC.

# Acknowledgments

Earlier versions of Starr's story and of the kayaker's story in "A Ferry and Four Keeper Holes," which were written in response to photographs by Whitney Ott, appeared as "Need" and "Wheel" on the flash fiction website Project 1:1000. An earlier version of "Going to Water on Wise Creek" appeared in Susurrus.

While writing these stories, I received generous moral, spiritual, and material support from more sources than I can name. I offer special thanks to my partner and co-pilgrim Pamela and to Emma, Micah, and Graham Johnston for their intrepid, hilarious spirits, for humoring my need for river, swamp, and trail time, and for being the first friends of my writing. Thank you to Eric O'Dell, whose painting graces the book cover, and to the many friends who paddled the Ocmulgee with me, some of them repeatedly, as the stories were taking shape. That list includes my partner Pam, Don Ream, Brett Toles, Wesley Rauls, Matt Harper, Doug Thompson, Eric O'Dell, Bill King, Michael Cass, and Andrew Bender. I'm grateful to Doug Thompson for valuable resources on African American river baptism and to Marc Jolley at Mercer University Press for his belief in the book. I'm also thankful to the College of Liberal Arts and Sciences at Mercer University for the sabbatical that let me complete the collection; to John Dunaway for a Lilly Fellowship that funded release time for drafting the first story; to Deneen Senasi, whose Faculty Research and Writing Colloquium at Mercer gave me valuable revision time; and to Ocmulgee Mounds National Historical Park, which welcomed me as artist in residence in 2012 and where the idea of an Ocmulgee River story cycle first came to me. Thank you to Kelley Land for skilled editing.

# The Only Place to Start From

Some sorry soul had gone to great lengths to steal the cart from Peavey's Publix, take it eight miles to the Spring Street bridge, wrestle it over the concrete rail, then drop it forty feet into the river below. It defied logic was what it did. It crossed out of the arena of minor chaos-causing that a grocery store manager dealt with daily and into outright malevolence—the invention of crime that didn't even pay.

The cop that called was Koenig, who had helped Peavey out a year ago when cases of maxipads and diapers had started disappearing from the check-in racks just inside the loading dock doors. Peavey owed him one for the two nights Koenig had spent staking out the stock room, and he sensed Koenig was calling him on it when he phoned about the cart in the creek. *Jimmy Carter is coming to talk at the college*, Koenig said. *The captain says he'll be crossing that bridge.* Peavey replied that it couldn't be his cart, not that far from his store. Koenig said he had personally seen Publix on the handlebar.

So here Peavey was in the meat manager's old Mazda pickup, rolling down Riverside Drive on buggy search and rescue. For the first fifteen minutes it felt fine, goosing down the open road in the middle of the morning (he hadn't driven a stick in ten years), the sunlight, not quite hot yet, slanting through the windshield. Then he turned off at the Riverwalk and saw the brown Ocmulgee, its width stretching twice as far as he could have thrown a football in his prime. A creek, Koenig had called it.

He should have brought a bag boy. He didn't remember that his youngest bag boy working that day was sixty-eight, which was why he hadn't asked him along.

Peavey backed the pickup down the boat ramp at the foot of the abutment and got out. The cart couldn't even be seen from the bridge above. Only the green handle and maybe four inches of the basket showed above the sluggish water just downstream of the nearest concrete pillar. A person would have to stand right at the bridge rail to spot it.

If he left it, Koenig would just keep calling—plus Peavey needed to stay on Koenig's good side. He thought about the shambling, long-haired teenagers who had been cruising up to Peavey's store on their skateboards from the movie theater down the strip mall, how they drifted in through the automatic doors and leaned their wet energy drink cans on the magazine racks as they read issues of *Thrasher* they never bought. Their bangs hid their eyes. There were little pieces of metal lodged in their faces like BBs.

Peavey had grabbed the pair of black, thigh-high rubber boots that were standing by the door of the store, placed there by the fire department to collect money for United Way. He dumped the contents of the left boot on the passenger seat—seventy-six pennies, nine receipts, eight nickels, six dimes, a Kit Kat wrapper, and a Spider-Man action figure missing an arm. The right boot held a dented can of baked beans, four receipts, a pair of thick reading glasses missing a lens, two one-dollar bills, an empty Pepsi bottle, and sixty-eight pennies. The tag was still on the reading glasses.

Peavey shed his Weejuns, poked his sock feet into the ridiculously high and heavy boots, and stepped into the river at the bottom of the ramp, heading for the cart handle. The water, mud brown when seen from the bridge, ran fairly clear in the shallows. Once Peavey was in it, each bootstep raised a small cloud of silt that immediately drifted downstream. There was more current than he had been able to see from the bridge. Rocks here and there cast shadows that told him how deep it was, at least for the first ten yards or so. Nervous minnows flicked away from him and then back. An aluminum can the sand had worn down to plain silver flashed under a ripple—his last glimpse of the bottom before the river rose to his knees and the current, moseying but unmistakably there, became a stiff headwind. Stepping blind, unsure of the depth until he committed himself, his right foot sank into a hole that scared him and therefore pissed him off. He bulled forward. Damn Koenig. The river shallowed for three steps, as if cowed, and then, on the fourth, just as he looked up at the cart not six feet away, his right toe struck a sunk log and he keeled over sideways.

The instant the boot-tops met the surface they sucked in gallons of river. A small step would have saved him, but his legs were heavy as lead. He fell—and felt such outrage that he was almost glad when he struck the surface full-body, only his head above the water. The river whacked him back with October cold that simultaneously burned his outsides and squeezed his insides. His lungs locked.

Peavey immediately struck bottom. He dug his hands into the fine sand and pushed himself up onto his knees, facing upstream, trying to plant a foot and stand. His boot, full and heavy as a bucket, went out from under him, rolling him onto his back. He thrashed, half sideways to the current, trying to set his heels in the shifting sand. Finally he wedged a sole against the very log that had dropped him in the first place and stood, the air searing him, his Publix vest, button-down, and polyesters plastered to his skin. Shorn of dignity, a complete catastrophe of retail management, he itched for somebody to fight or fire.

Gasping with cold, he wrestled the boots off, dumped them, then stepped back into them, feeling sand grate through his socks. The river had all it wanted from him: in two easy steps he could grab the buggy by its front grille.

It was sunk in some kind of hole. He had to bend down to grab it and tug. It didn't budge. He seized the rim of the basket and pulled hard with his back, not using his knees as the stock room safety posters dictated. The cart moved not an inch, but something inside it did—a shadow two shades greener than the water rose, as long and thick as an arm, blunt-snouted. Peavy stared into a flat, undead eye above an open jaw filled like a comb with teeth.

He leapt backward, too short of breath for a real shout, though he shot out a loud *Gaw*—half a *God*, maybe. A bolt of panic buzzed through him as his heel kicked the same log

4

again. He barely managed to save himself from a second baptism.

Peavey leaned over the cart, careful not to step any closer. It wasn't a snake, unless an eel was a snake. It hove to the surface, slow as a fogged-in zeppelin—a fish that almost filled the cart diagonally, its fins fingering the water. It pointed downstream steady and level as a compass needle, the long, toothy jaws slightly open. It looked a little stupid, the head absurdly small in proportion to the rest of the body and like a living pair of oversized needle-nose pliers.

Peavey didn't know fish at all, unless you counted the dead ones people bought out of the ice-filled case at the back of the store. Once, four years ago, he had had to lift a live lobster out of a tank with tongs because his seafood manager had been at the hospital with his wife, who was having a baby. The lobster had rubber bands cuffing its claws. This fish in the grocery cart looked predatory and prehistoric—armored, pea-brained, vaguely barracudic. Certainly it was no bream, bass, catfish, or carp. He had seen these, which older folks—often old black women—had tried to sell to him.

It could be the last of its kind. Tomorrow's *Telegraph* headline scrolled across his brain: "Publix's Peavey Lands Living Fossil." He leaned a little closer to the cart rim.

*He ain't yours.*

The voice made Peavey start spastically. He looked up into the rafters of the bridge, trying to spot who was talking.

*He ain't your fish,* the voice repeated. There was a head, a face peering over the concrete railing of the bridge, so dark against the sky that Peavey couldn't see the features. Whoever it was had a ball cap on.

*Then why is he in my cart?* Peavey answered, glad for the first time that he had worn his aqua vest, soaked, but with his gold plastic name tag on it.

*Don't you touch him 'fore I get down there.* The face disappeared.

Peavey knew he should get out of the river before this mystery person got between him and the truck, but part of him had its hackles up. The truth of what he had just said—it *was* his cart—threaded up his spine. He took two ruefully careful steps toward the bank before a tall, skinny scarecrow rounded the end of the bridge guardrail and came down the embankment in a slow-motion lope. White t-shirt, a formerly dark blue Braves cap faded to a dusty purplish color, jeans with one knee worn to white threads—he was a kid, fifteen at the outside. The scarecrow threw a glance through the open door of the pickup as he passed it. He didn't stop until he reached the bottom of the ramp.

*Just you leave the buggy till I get him out of it,* the kid said. His voice seemed smaller now that Peavy could pair a body with it.

*I'm not wading back out here again.*

*It looks more like you swimmed.*

Peavey watched him. It was a hard face to read—sallow skin, narrow eyes, that cap pulled down—was he smirking? Peavey fell back on the bluster he used on the skate kids in the store.

6

*Where are your parents? Do they know you've been stealing grocery carts?*

*I didn't steal nothing. It was sitting up there by the bridge two whole days. Probably saved a car from hitting it.*

*You see what it says on that handle? It's mine.*

*Your name is Publix?*

Peavey snorted and turned back toward the cart. He pushed at it as if he were trying to tip it and free the fish.

*You know you left your keys in here?*

Peavey looked back. The boy was standing just inside the door of the Mazda on the boat ramp.

*I'll back it out there to you. It don't look all that deep.*

*You stay away from that truck.*

*It's all right. I've drove before.* The boy was easing his long leg under the steering wheel.

*No!* The boy looked back at Peavey. *Fine. Come get your fish. Get your fish, and then you get my cart out of the goddang river and we'll just call it even.*

*All right. Deal.* The boy stepped out of the truck and started toward the embankment.

*Where are you going?*

*I can't get him with my hands.*

The boy loped up the boat ramp across the empty drive, not hurrying. He entered the shade under a stand of young trees on the other side of the asphalt, then came back out into the sun and down the ramp with two long sticks in his left hand. As he approached, Peavey saw that one was forked at the end like a slingshot. The other was sharpened to a faceted yellow point like a big, leadless pencil.

Peavey's neck prickled. *You stop right there.*

*It's okay,* the boy said. *I know the way.*

He walked right in, jeans and all. Rather than bearing toward Peavy and the cart, he sloshed upriver five or six strides, then stepped on rocks just under the surface until he arrived upstream of the buggy's green cage. Knee deep, he slowly worked his way down to it. An arm's length away, the boy stopped and poked the forked stick into the water at the tail of the cart.

*Got to close the door so he don't wiggle out. If I get after him with the spear he'll go down and out that crack he come in through.*

There was movement in the cart. It dawned on Peavey that this boy had caught this fish on purpose—had trapped it in a grocery buggy.

The kid drew his forked stick out of the water and moved slowly toward the cart. Using the forked stick in his right hand as a pole to steady himself against the bottom, he raised the other, sharpened stick in his left. Everything but the current seemed to hold still around him. The boy froze for a long minute.

Just as Peavey opened his mouth to complain, the same shadow as before came wavering to the surface inside the cart's rim. In the flick of a second, the butt of the spear was clattering against the metal grillwork of the buggy, scribbling circles in the air over the water. In four beats it stopped, the shaft coming to rest at a downstream slant against the top of the cart, the wet bark on the spear so black it looked purple.

The boy gripped the stick and raised the fish out of the water. The point had gone all the way through just behind the gills. It looked smaller in the air, and dead, but also brutally beautiful. It had vivid dark spots on it and a rich gloss.

*Not a 'gator gar. They hard to find now. But he's nice.* The fish's tail curled slightly at the compliment.

Peavey looked at the scales skeptically. The boy noticed.

*Them would make some nice points, yeah? Just right for a length of cane.*

*It doesn't look edible.*

*I wouldn't eat him. Not 'less I was a sight hungrier than I am now. Bones in every mouse-bite of him.*

*If you're not going to eat it—*

*We don't eat gar fish. Don't eat any fish, much. Not when there's better.*

*Then why didn't you just let it go?*

The boy's almond-shaped eyes narrowed. He looked harder at Peavey than he had so far.

*I'm just curious*, Peavey said.

The kid seemed to be weighing something in his head.

*You party to it, so I guess you can know*, he said. *I need the teeth.*

*The teeth?*

*To make my marks. Be a man.*

*Your marks.*

*That there's about enough talk, Mr. Publix. Too much talk'll mess it all up.* He poked the handle of the stick at Peavey. *Hold him a minute and I'll get you your buggy.*

Peavey stood there with a fish on a stick while the boy waded to the cart, coming at it from upriver as before. The boy gripped the handle and pulled upstream. It came grudgingly free.

*It's a perfect little vee for a weir right there,* the boy called to him. *Just chucked me a couple of good-sized rocks around her.*

The boy wrestled the cart through the water, the wheels digging up swirling, latte-colored clouds of silt. In the shallows, Peavey saw the cart held a wide, flat, ink-black stone as big as a hubcap. The boy pried it up and forearmed it out of the basket, dropping it into the rill of water near the bank, then started working the buggy along until he had the front wheels on the boat ramp.

*I'll get it from here.*

*Deal was, I'd get it out for you. Watch out, now.* The boy circled around to the handle and pushed and lifted at the same time so that the rear wheels went up onto the cement. He rattled the cart over to the truck. It didn't look any the worse for wear. Peavey sloshed out of the river, holding the pierced fish in one hand while he dropped the tailgate of the truck with the other. Once his boot met pavement, he felt a mild, alarming quiver in the spear.

The boy rared back against the weight of the cart, raising it into the truck bed and laying it on its side. Wet, green, and skeletal, it looked like a fish trap. Peavey slammed the tailgate and handed over the spear.

*Thanks.*

*You're welcome. Thank you, too—for getting the cart.*

The boy started up the ramp.

*You need a ride somewhere?*

The boy looked back at Peavey. *You got your marks?*

*What?*

*She said ask the helper, so I'm asking.*

*Asking what? Who said?*

*I can't ask it twice.*

*I don't know what you mean, my marks.*

*Then you don't have them. If you got them you know.*

*I got marks all right.*

*Then you ought to know without me saying.*

*I've got to get back to work.*

The boy turned. *Bye, Mr. Publix.*

*Who? Who said?*

*The grandmother. She said there'd be a helper. You didn't seem like one at first but then you did, sort of.*

*Forget the marks. I'll still give you a ride.*

*The teeth makes marks. Take his jawbone, some soot for ink. Like a tattoo.*

*That's not sanitary.*

*Is so. Soot's from fire.*

*Fish teeth, though—you know what's in that water?*

*Never mind.* The boy looked at the fish, utterly still now on its spear. *You ain't the helper.* He turned and started up the grassy bank beside the ramp, ambling toward the sidewalk that ran downstream and away from the bridge, the fish bouncing a little on the stick as he went, the kid's back straight as a flagpole.

*You can still have the ride,* Peavey called after him.

*No thanks. I got to do this right.* The boy looked at the sun. *I got until noon.* He started walking.

❧

Peavey couldn't stand it. He wanted to be the helper. It irked him to want it, but he did. He got in the truck and spun the wheels a little in outrage so that he bounced going up the ramp. Rather than heading toward the store he drove down to the Second Street bridge, crossed, and pulled over just past its far end, his hazards blinking. It wasn't four minutes before he saw the boy, below and on the opposite bank of the river, making long strides along the concrete sidewalk with his stuck fish until he disappeared under the far end of the bridge. Peavey got out of the truck, crossed the bridge, and looked downstream. Though the riverside park and sidewalk ended under the bridge, the boy was still making his way downriver, going much slower as he pushed through the trees and brush on the steep bank.

Peavey was on the last bridge in town. The kid must be camping, must have a tent on the bank. Peavey tried to re-member where the river went, what was on this side, the east one, opposite downtown. The west bank he knew, vaguely— a levee walled off the river from the ball fields at the park where the store-sponsored softball team lost half its games every spring. Interstate 16 was all he knew of on the east side where the boy was walking. Peavey had driven 16 to Savannah but had never looked away from the road.

There were the old Indian mounds and the state park around them. He had been once, years ago, filling in for an assistant manager on a catering job, but had no idea whether the park stretched all the way down to the river.

In two turns, maybe three miles, Peavey ended up at the park. He made a right off the four-lane just past the housing project, and it was as if the city had evaporated. The road rose through oak and pine woods, dipped into a field with a white farmhouse nestled in it, then passed an art-deco visitor's center. After that the woods closed in on both shoulders. He saw a metal sign the same brown color as everything else you saw in these places: ← River Trail. He parked below a big, flat-topped hill and went where the sign pointed.

Peavey had nothing against nature, but he mostly stayed out of it. The way the path wove through the woods made him heady, edgy, then heady again. He crossed a sunny, open swamp on a long, curving boardwalk, surprising two ducks he was pretty sure were wild, since they weren't white. Lily pads, cloudless blue sky. The woods closed around the boardwalk as it led onto a damp dirt trail that tunneled through a thicket. Peavey thought about bears and alligators.

He kept going, his wet clothes registering the chill in the deep shade under the trees. The susurrus of the interstate calmed him. The path turned sandy and fell in alongside a steep-banked, smelly creek, then emerged from the woods to pass under the elevated highway: the axels of a log truck boomed across the roadbed over his head. Not long after passing under the traffic, he came out of the trees at the river, wide and brown across a beach of dry, rusty sand. The sun warmed his shoulders after the shade of the woods.

Peavey climbed a rise of sand that leveled off on top to see farther upstream. Four rocks had been planted there as if at the corners of a square. Four lengths of driftwood had been laid so that their ends met in a cross at the square's center.

*≈*

He was still looking at it when he heard the crash of brush upstream and glimpsed above it first the gar, then the boy's Braves cap, bobbing toward him through the low willows and scrub. The kid came out of the brush and side-stepped down the bank to the beach, showing no surprise when he saw Peavey sitting on the sandy swell.

*Sorry I took so long,* the boy said. *It's all growed up between there and here.* He stabbed the blunt end of his spear, the gar still on its tip, into the sand. *You could of got more wood together.*

*You want it here?*

*By the rocks, please.*

Inland Peavey found a dead branch thick as a baseball bat tangled up and hanging in some vines, yanked until he got it down, and dragged it to the beach. He gathered an armload of pine limbs, piling them beside the stones. The dead branches broke up easily. A breeze sprang up under the trees, chilling him again.

At the sandbar, the boy looked up at the sun where it burned over the treetops, then he stooped and from a pile alongside the cross he took stringy gray hanks of Spanish moss and wove them under and over the crux ends of the driftwood. Peavey thought of macramé.

Done with the weaving, the boy piled tinder in the gap where the logs almost met. Near the pile he set one rock between each of the four logs, then squatted, opening a knife from the pocket of his enormous jeans and shaving long curls of bark off a stick into the center of the twigs and moss.

Peavey was both chilled and greased with sweat. The boy's face when he sat down in the sand was dry as a leaf.

*So now you're going to light that? Bring the park rangers down all over us?*

The boy only raised his shoulders then dropped them.

*What is all this? Who are you?*

*This is your place. You should say your name first.*

*I thought my name was Publix.*

The boy grinned. He pushed his cap back. Under it he had a black, kinky buzz cut. Peavey felt a small shock. He had expected long black hair.

*This isn't my place,* Peavey said. *I've never been here before.*

*So you giving it back, then?*

Peavey plucked at his gold plastic name tag. *Darrell. Darrell Peavey.*

*John Mark.*

*John Mark what?*

*Just John Mark.*

*And you're doing what?*

*Waiting on the fire. Same as you.*

*I carried all that wood down here and you don't have a match?*

*I didn't say I didn't have no match.*

*Well do you?*

*I have to wait for the fire.*

*You have to wait for the fire. What—lightning?*

*That would be one way, Darrell.*

*Mr. Peavey.*

*Mr. Peavey.*

*You don't have a prayer, kid.*

*Do you have a prayer, Mr. Peavey?*

*What?*

*Never mind. All this is the prayer.*

They sat. The kid said nothing. Didn't even close his eyes.

Peavey stood up. *I have a grocery store to go run.*

He left the boy sitting there cross-legged between the water and the woods. He followed the path back to the parking lot, trying to be angry but too tired.

෴

As soon as he opened the door of the truck he caught it—a smell familiar but so out of place he couldn't recognize it for a second: the sharp smolder of the heat gun they used in the store deli to shrink-wrap trays of cheese and cold cuts.

His eye found the source: a faint tendril of smoke rose from a spot of rainbow on the vinyl of the passenger seat. Peavey's eye followed the focused beam of sun backward from the prismatic blur on the seat to the surviving lens of the reading glasses perched on the dashboard.

ॐ

John Mark stood up when Peavey came down the bank and across the beach.

*This ain't just any old fire*, he said. *It's to remember the first one. It's new and clean. All the other fires in this place will be lit from this one.*

Peavey held up the glasses. John Mark grinned. He took off his cap. The hair down the crown of his buzz cut was long and gathered in a dark, frizzy knot the size of a kiwi.

Peavey offered the frames. John Mark stepped back, his hands in his pockets.

*What? Are these against the rules?* Peavey asked.

*It's ways, not rules*, John Mark said. *You go right on and try.*

*It's not my place*, Peavey said.

*You keep saying that. Some helper you are.* He grinned again. *You're right here, where it all meets. You belong to the place.*

Peavey looked at the crossed logs with their sharpened ends. They reminded him of a compass drawn on an old map.

*I get it now. The four directions.*

*Not four. Seven,* John Mark said. *You're forgetting up and down.*

*That's six.*

*Right here, right now.*

*How is that a direction?*

John Mark shrugged. *It's the only place to start from.*

Peavey squatted at the nest for the fire, holding the glasses this way and that at different angles to the noon sun until a mottle of primary colors wobbled on the curls of bark in the center of the pile. He held the frames still, watching. The bright spot began to blacken the soft wood. When smoke started winding up from the pile, the boy leaned and blew. A flame flashed up, quivering. Peavey sat back, watching the boy's back as he nursed the fire.

∿

The dream Peavey had was a shallow one, taking place where he sat, on that very sand and by that very fire at that very time of day. His foot was pinned under four green logs with the store logo on them. A blaze had been set to burn him out of this trap by someone who had just left but was (Peavey was sure) coming back. The returner (Peavey was sure) would bring a gar-tooth saw.

When he woke from the doze, Peavey thought for the first two seconds that the man standing in front of him in ball cap and sunglasses was the returner. For the second two seconds he thought the man was John Mark.

*Saw?* Peavey asked.

*Saw? Saw what?*

Hearing the voice, Peavey took in the green uniform and the loaded-down belt—neat black cases, a pistol holstered on the right hip.

*Sir, did you start this fire?*

*Yes. No. I mean, not alone. I helped.*

*Helped who, sir?*

*The boy.* Peavey looked around. John Mark was nowhere to be seen. *There was a boy here with me. An Indian boy, I think.*

*Have you been swimming, sir?*

*No.* Peavey looked down at his wet clothes. *I fell in earlier, trying to get my grocery cart out.*

*And the fish?*

*The fish isn't mine. I'm watching it for the boy. He caught it with my cart, though.*

*Sir, it's a crime to kill anything in a wildlife refuge—fish included.*

*I didn't kill it. He did.*

*Fires are also illegal in a refuge. Maybe you didn't see the signs. Maybe you and the boy didn't, I mean—if he was old enough to read.*

*You think I'm making this up.*

The ranger regarded the toe of his black boot. He looked more and more like a cop—said *sir* the same way Koenig had said it to the stockboy who'd stolen the diapers.

*You think I'm crazy. Look in my truck. The cart is there.*

*What truck is that, sir?*

*In the parking lot back up the river trail, next to the big hill.*

*I think you mean the temple mound.*

*Yes.*

*I came from that way. The lot was empty.*

*I was just there.*

*Do you have some ID, sir? So I know who I'm talking to?*

*I'm Darrell Peavey. My driver's license is in my wallet in the truck.*

But the truck was gone, as Peavey saw when the ranger called in his partner, who drove them in a sort of militarized golf cart with knobby tires back to the parking lot and stopped.

*The boy must have taken it,* Peavey said.

*The Native boy, you mean?*

*Yes.*

*Can you describe the Native boy, sir?*

*Braves cap, white shirt, old jeans. He said his name was John Mark.*

*And he said he was Native American?*

*He looked like he was. I mean, he acted like he was. He speared that gar.*

*I thought you said he caught it.*

*He caught it, then he speared it.*

The other ranger broke in to ask the model of the missing pickup.

*It was an older Mazda. Orange.*

*What year?*

*I don't know.*

The rangers looked at each other.

*It wasn't mine. I borrowed it. To get the cart out of the river. You guys have to find it.*

*You know, sir, I think you need to talk to the superintendent.* He turned to his partner. *Ray, go back and keep an eye on that fire. I'll drive him to the center.*

The ranger who had waked him took him to the visitor's center, the low buff building Peavey had passed coming into the park. In the museum inside, among clear cases of spear points and clay pots, Peavey caught sight of a diorama behind glass and stopped: there was a fire in the center of a kind of courtyard between lean-tos, the ends of four logs meeting where a plastic flame burned. Two brown action figures with whited faces stood on either side of it, their arms raised. They looked as if they were singing. One of the two had chains of small spots along his arms and on his shoulders and neck. The figure had the same buzz cut as John Mark and a thicker version of his hair knot.

*The boy had hair just like that,* Peavey said. *He laid out the logs for the fire that way, too.*

*Yes, sir. You can tell the super all about it.*

He sat Peavey in a break room at a folding table, where he waited long enough to begin to wish he had change for the soda and snack machines. His worries about the truck gradually gave way to a confidence that the rangers were already getting it back. Why else would he be cooling his heels like this? On a bulletin board was a neat grid of policies, pictures of invasive species—tallow tree, Chinese privet, wisteria, wild hogs—and a slightly blurry photo of a bobcat on the slope of one of the mounds.

After twenty minutes, Peavey cracked the door open and found the ranger who had waked him up standing outside.

*Sorry for the wait, sir. Only a few more minutes.*

He should have them call Koenig. Koenig would tell them about President Carter and the grocery cart. He would confirm enough of Peavey's story to get him out of here and back to the store. But Koenig wouldn't be happy about it—and there was still a slim hope that Peavey would get out of all this without dealing with the police or trying to explain the buggy, the speared gar, the fire, or the missing truck to the district manager. Peavey had said too much to the rangers—had sounded crazy. What had he been thinking? He began to organize the story in his head, to practice telling it so that he would sound sane when the superintendent came in. He had been conned by the boy, who had obviously been after the truck all along. Peavey had only tried to help.

When the superintendent shuffled in, short and wearing small octagonal glasses that made him every age between forty-five and sixty, he paused only long enough to shake Peavey's hand and apologize for his wait before asking Peavey to follow him. They went down a set of stairs and out a steel door to a parking lot that must have been behind the building.

Where Peavey had hoped the truck (and feared a squad car) would be, there was only the golf cart. The superintendent waved Peavey onto the front seat and took Peavey's former seat on the back himself. The ranger who had found Peavey on the sand bar drove. They set off down an asphalt path through the woods behind the visitor's center.

The cart crossed a plank bridge over a creek and labored up a sparsely wooded hill. Coming to a high fence topped with razor wire, the ranger driving followed it, leaving the asphalt path behind so that they trundled down a right-of-way alongside the chain link.

They topped a rise and turned away from the fence toward the base of a small mound, going slower than before. As they rounded the earthwork, they came up beside the chain link again, following it until it met another fence to form a corner which the mound nestled inside.

The cart stopped. Down the slope on the other side of the fence was a neighborhood of many small identical block houses, all the same shade of brown, all with the same clotheslines in the same bald backyards, the same square back stoops. The houses filled the hollow at the bottom of the hill and ascended another rise beyond it.

*Is that your truck, Mr. Peavey?*

Peavey followed the superintendent's eye to the corner of a house below them and to the right. The grill and a corner of the Mazda's hood were just visible beyond the edge of the house.

*It looks like it.*

*If you don't mind, we'll sit here for a bit—see who comes out of the house.*

*What if he tries to take off in it when he comes out? It's not my truck.*

*I don't think he will, Mr. Peavey. The boy you met was light complected, was he not? With a topknot? I thought so. He is known to us.*

*That's his house?*

*His grandmother's.*

*So he's done this before?*

*He has not, no. He has an active imagination that he has put into action in other ways.*

*He cons people, doesn't he? The people who come to the park?*

*Oh, no, no. He isn't wicked. Mischievous, rather. A touch confused. He is a voracious reader.*

The ranger driving snorted.

*Excuse Jerry, who no doubt wants me to admit that the boy has stolen books from our gift shop. That would be where he found the names John and Mark, the names Hernando de Soto's friars gave to two Hitchiti boys they baptized in the Ocmulgee. The boy has read parts of Rodrigo Ranjel's chronicle of Soto's travels through here. Jerry himself would have to admit that the Ranjel book, like every book he has taken, was eventually returned.*

*So you think he is going to return the pickup?*

*Yes. He thinks of ownership in terms of need. Tools are communal property. They belong to those who need them the most for as long as they need them. He gets this from his reading.*

*So he isn't Indian?*

*He tries to be. As I said, he is a voracious reader.*

*So he reads these books you were talking about and then, what—imitates them?*

24

The superintendent said nothing, only went on looking down the hill at the truck.

*Did Indians return horses after they stole them?*

*The Muscogee did not steal horses. The Plains nations did that—and, no, they did not return them.*

*If your horse was stolen you went and stole it back,* Jerry said.

Peavey looked at the superintendent, who shrugged.

*You're telling me to just go over there and get it?*

Again the superintendent said nothing.

*That way there's no stolen car to report to the cops, right?*

The superintendent didn't look at Peavey, but Jerry did.

*That way there's no charges to file against grown men who spear animals, start fires, and swim in their clothes in a federal wildlife refuge.*

*Oh.*

*The answer to your next question,* Jerry said, *is no, I will not go over there with you.*

୬

Peavey wasn't prepared for the snick of the lock behind him after Jerry let him through the gate. It sounded as small and sharp as the cock of a pistol, but he was damned if he was going to give Jerry the satisfaction of a single minute's hesitation. Peavey headed straight for the truck, striding across the grass briskly as he did in the store when he needed to get past an irate customer or a needy soft drink supplier trying to wheedle an endcap out of him.

Peavey didn't stop until he rounded the corner of the house. The truck was loaded down with liquor boxes, a trunk, an upholstered rocker. Seeing this brought Peavey up short, vaporizing his hope that he would find the key in the ignition where he could simply turn it and go.

A side door into the house opened and John Mark leaned out.

*Some helper you are,* he said. *The heavy stuff's all in there already.*

*Thief.*

*Indian giver.*

*I ought to call the cops.*

*The cops is the one's brought you.* John Mark waved past Peavey, who turned in time to see Jerry and the superintendent rolling away on the golf cart.

*Park rangers aren't cops. Not real ones.*

*I bet you didn't say that to them.*

*This is outside their jurisdiction.*

*Yeah. So you're safe now. Back on the reservation.*

*They told me about you. You can quit the act.*

*I'm not acting, Mr. Peavey. What you do is who you are.*

*A thief steals.*

*I thought you was offering. Helping.*

*You ran off as soon as my back was turned—with a truck that isn't even mine.*

*If it ain't yours, how can I be stealing it from you?*

*Just quit with the double talk and give me the key.*

*The key is in it.*

*Get that stuff out of the back.*

*It ain't got to where it's going yet.*

*It's not going anywhere in my truck.*

*So now it is yours.*

*I'm responsible for it.*

*Like I'm responsible for the grandmother. For her stuff that's* in there.

*So you're moving her?*

*I told you. I'm getting my marks. This is one of the steps.*

*Moving her where?*

*Oklahoma.* The boy laughed. *Just kidding. Two streets* over.

They looked at each other. Peavey remembered his dad's late-night Westerns—an Italian actor in red makeup saying the White man speaks with a forked tongue.

*Where is she?*

*Gone already.*

*Gone where?*

*You don't believe in the grandmother?*

*You keep saying* the *when you should say* my.

*So now you're claiming the grandmother, too?*

*Your* my, *not my* my.

My *my? My my.*

Peavey bit his lips together.

*Your goat is got, ain't it? See how it's better not to have your own personal goat in the first place? I can't do nothing for* my *grandmother. But* the *grandmother—that's different.*

*Is that something from one of those books you stole?*

*Sort of. The books don't get it right.*

*They don't. Do tell me.*

*Ain't nothing anybody's, really. You get trusted with something, that's all. For a limited time only.*

*Like the truck.*

*Yes.*

*Like my store that I need to get back to.*

*Yes. That you can go straight back to once you've helped.*

Peavey didn't say *Like these Muscogee ways you're cribbing.*

John Mark stepped back inside the door and handed out a box. Against his better judgment, Peavey accepted it, then another and another after it, until he had filled the truck bed and the passenger seat. When there was no room left for another box, Peavey went to the door and spoke through the screen.

*That's it. Full up.*

There was no reply. No lights were on and the house was strangely dark for midday. Peavey walked to the back of the truck and peered around the corner of the house to check the front yard.

Along the curb a loose string of people—six women or older girls, half as many men—stood watching the front door. Startled and uneasy, Peavey stepped back the way he had come. His sense of solitariness returned.

He opened the screen door into a cramped, dark kitchen, the worn counters empty. He crossed the concrete floor into a narrow hallway, passing a closed door on his right. The next door stood open on a tight bedroom. There was a small, chipped desk under a curtained window, a twin bed tidily made up with a thin blue bedspread, a nightstand of two milk crates with a lamp and a radio tape player on top of it, an old toy box with cowboys riding broncos and firing pistols. There was a bookcase of planks on concrete blocks. A few plastic planets hung by fishing line from the low ceiling. There were posters of a wolf and a slam-dunking basketball player on the wall. Except for a few gaps in the shelves where books had been taken, Peavey could see that nothing from this room was packed. He felt his anger begin to rise again.

He turned back down the hall, coming at its end to another bedroom (empty). Across the hall through another door, he saw a living room, nothing in it except an old vinyl loveseat with a slash of silver tape across one cushion—and Peavey's shopping cart.

The horn on the truck blew twice, briefly. Peavey hurried down the hall and back outside, sure the kid would be backing down the drive. Instead, John Mark stood by the driver-side door, a hand on the open window frame.

*Figured you had done had enough of me driving.*

*Where's the grandmother?*

*Gone on before. You go 'round the curve right there, then take your second right. Stop at the fourth house on the right.*

*You're walking?*

*I can't fit in there with all that stuff. You just pull up in front. There's people there.*

At least the kid didn't expect Peavey to pack up that bedroom. Peavey would go, drop this load, then get back to the store. As he backed out past the poker-faced crowd on the curb, he gave the kid credit for having the sense not to leave the last load unguarded.

The new place was identical to the old, except for a skinny tree in the front yard. Three men in light blue uniform shirts and work pants started lifting the boxes out of the truck bed before Peavey had turned the engine off. He didn't even have to get out. They ferried the whole load up the sidewalk and into the house like a very slow line of ants. Afterward, the biggest of the men—he had a gut and a walrus mustache—told Peavey to wait for him. Fifteen minutes later he came back and stuck a clipboard through the window at Peavey.

*Sign the bottom. Write down the value if you want to take it off your taxes.*

*It's not my stuff. And it's being moved, not donated.*

*It's all donations here, mister.*

They looked at each other.

*Your own personal goat.*

*Say what?*

*Nothing.* Peavey signed and handed the board back. *Thanks.*

ↄ

There was no sign of the boy as Peavey drove back the way he had come. Two men carried a mattress along the sidewalk. A skinny girl with beads in her hair had Jupiter and Saturn in the crook of one arm and a radio tape player hanging from a strap over her other shoulder.

At the grandmother's, the front door stood open. In the next yard over, a grizzled old man in a too-big tank-top undershirt carried one end of the loveseat while a boy not ten years old struggled with the other.

Inside, Peavey found the boy's bedroom, like the rest of the house, stripped bare. Only the wolf poster was left. He pushed a finger under the corners, prying up the tape from the cinderblock wall, careful not to tear the paper. It came down easily.

With the curtains gone and the wolf rolled into a tube in Peavey's hand, the room was blank and too bright. He left.

Crossing the yard to the truck, he smelled newspaper burning. Turning, he saw a ghost of smoke drift low to the ground from behind the house.

He found the boy feeding the pages of a last book into a small fire. The boy looked up as Peavey approached.

*That's either a blowgun or my poster.*

Peavey handed it over. John Mark accepted it, then blew through it onto the flames, which swirled up, carrying weightless black flakes of pages into the air. The boy planted it in the middle of the fire like a flag. He sighed.

*I was hoping one of them kids would take it.*

*They took everything else. Like vultures.*

*They waited real polite.*

*Buzzards.*

*The people that used to live here, they said a buzzard made the world.*

*Why let them take your things?*

31

*Burning them was going to hurt something awful. It hurts, watching the new fire burning up the old things.*

*You saved your grandmother's stuff.*

*For her friends. For people who need stuff. So she can go on with them. That purifies, too.*

Peavey felt himself starting to understand. *I'm sorry.*

*The people don't talk about that. To talk about somebody gone calls them back. They get confused about where they belong, who their people are.*

White smoke poured from the rolled poster like a smokestack.

*Come back to the river with me, if you want. Get your marks.*

*I don't know about marks, but I'll drive you back over there.*

*I have to walk.*

*You can't. Jerry locked the gate.*

*He unlocked it when they brung me the fire.*

*They brought you fire?*

*Ain't but one pure fire. All fires have got to start from that one.* He held up a blackened pottery bowl. *They brung me a coal. I got to wait a while. Bring some of this ash back with me.*

*For your marks.*

*Yes, sir.*

*What if the one fire goes out?*

*The people don't talk about that, neither.*

Peavey went back to the truck and climbed in, intent on getting back to the riverside, keeping the embers going. Pulling out of the housing project, he saw the old gray man who had been carrying one end of the loveseat. He was slowly pushing the shopping cart up the street. Peavey decided to trust him with it, for a limited time only.

# Burying Ground

The Wednesday after his stroke, Nicodemus came to church for the first time in thirty years. Tobit was as surprised as everybody else. Ruby, who had found Demus and gotten him to the doctor, had been taking care of him, and Tobit figured she had made him come. Ruby took her usual pew halfway down the left side of the aisle while Demus hung back. Tobit watched him slowly take a seat on the ushers' pew just inside the vestibule, where he passed the service frowning at the opposite wall, never looking toward the pulpit. Demus didn't blink his eyes that Tobit saw, nor did he rise for the hymns or the reading of the gospel, but on the first word of the first verse of the invitation, Demus shakily stood and began the long shuffle toward the altar. He was born again with one foot in the grave.

The stroke had slowed him, but he was still Demus, still fierce. He wouldn't be baptized at all unless it was at the old burying grounds where his mother and brother had gone under, and so the very next day, before Demus grew any poorer in body, Tobit tried to take off work to search out the right spot on the river. The old grounds were a neighborhood now, with a guard and a gate.

Tobit couldn't afford the time off, but this was soul business, one of those times that tested whether a man was the Lord's, and so he asked. Mr. Peavey said no. Said the store needed Tobit, all the last Halloween things to put up and the first Thanksgiving displays to unpack. To hear him talk, you would have thought a line of trucks full of stuffing and canned cranberries was idling at the loading dock.

That left only Sunday. Tobit rued disrespecting the Sabbath, but the ox was in the ditch. Demus could up and die. A cold snap could kill him.

And so Tobit took the bus as far north of town as it went, to the new shopping center with the big bookstore in it, and from there he walked north and east with his King James under his arm along the road toward the river. He hadn't been up there near the dam in twenty years. The last trip had been for a baptizing, too, but an indoors one in a little clapboard house made into a church by some Pentecostals. A preacher from over in Alabama had showed up with a rattlesnake, which was when Tobit had got out of there. He had been supposed to play the bass and get paid for it out of a love offering. Jesus said it his own self: Do not put the Lord your God to the test.

This Sunday was God's own day for walking. Pretty as you please with the maples showing themselves in that red only a maple has, making the sycamore that much yellower. The knee-high grass on the shoulder wet the hem of his suit pants when he tried to walk there, so he stayed between the white line and the road edge, thinking of it as a way laid for him, which is also how he thought of it when the pickup truck passed him, slowed, then backed up, and the man inside offered him a ride. The way laid for you you take, Tobit's daddy always said. You would know it when you came to it.

They didn't talk much, just *how you* and *ain't it pretty*. There was church on the radio—one of those big organ churches downtown having communion, folks probably sipping real wine, which Tobit didn't hold with, out of a big cup. Tobit felt bad for missing services, then worse hearing the words of the Lord's Supper but not tasting the broken cracker, not answering back in the responsive reading.

*You a preacher?* the man asked.

*No, sir. I go to preaching.*

*Seen your Bible there.*

*It's a help to me, that's all. Shows me my way.*

*A good map, is it.*

*Brought me this far.*

*So I see. You going to preaching now?*

*No, sir. Called away this morning.*

*Bet you don't miss many Sundays.*

*My work keeps me away some.*

*That ain't right.*

*The spirit's there, too. You don't ever know. Where a body is is where they're called to be.*

*Well. Wish the Lord'd told my boy that instead of calling him to Iraq.*

Tobit kept quiet.

*Claimed he got the call in church.*

*Your boy in the army?*

*He was.*

They rode on in silence.

*Right up yonder at that turnoff will be fine, please sir.*

Tobit and the man waved once at each other, went their ways.

ے

The way to the river was paved now. Tobit hadn't known he was looking forward to walking down the old dirt road until he set his shoes on the coarse gray asphalt. Pavement was hard on the feet. Hot. Road clay, though, had a smell to make a body just want to walk.

As it gradually sloped down toward the river, the road entered the shade of the woods. He began to pass small houses and trailers, old but tended to, mostly. He kept his eyes on the asphalt but saw from the corner of his eye a stack of used lumber up on blocks beneath one trailer and, under an old tin roof, plastic drums and empty milk jugs strung on twine. There were still saving-up people out here, people tuned in to providence.

After the seventh house, he passed the town—a few houses and storefronts and a clapboard post office, all of it on the right side of the road along a single side street. The gas station and store had been made into a café, though it still had its old motor oil and Royal Crown Cola signs. Tobit was pleased to see that it was closed. Behind the town on the near bank of the river stood the tall brick mill, most of its windows broken out and trumpet creeper climbing its walls. The shell of the place saddened him. The last time he had been through here, Tobit had sat across the river listening to the hum of the looms, watching motes of cotton fuzz drift from the mill's open windows in a sort of fog. He had thought about working there, trying for a job, but during the shift change, seeing many faces both coming out and going in, he had known there was no place for him hereabouts.

The road, banked up level, shot out over a long bridge. On the downstream side he could see only the horizon line across the river, wide and seemingly still where it spilled over the dam. It looked like the edge of the world, a border where the slow, deep, black-green river ceased in midair. His ears knew better, picking up the steady shush of the spillway falls that stretched from bank to bank and marked the place where the river leapt down, remembered itself, and went on changed—fast, rocky, shallow. Loud, too. A gladness rose up in him. He crossed the bridge quickly, feeling how his dark suit coat drew the sun. The warm weather felt like a sign.

The old river made him work to get to her down below the dam. He was a half hour poking around in bogs, witch hazel, and yellowing head-high grass before he returned to the road, which took him winding through some ruined mill houses, two without doors, and one old roofless stone silo. Then the pavement gave way to sandy dirt and the heavy smell of muddy banks and water slicking over rock.

He followed a path arched over by a privet thicket, moist air moving under the cuffs of his pants. There he stood on the bank, at the fork where the deeper, swifter channel from the dam's small powerhouse met the wider, rockier main stream. He was a long stone-skip below the dam, visible through a stand of young trees on the tongue of land between the channels. The water foamed white at the tailrace. He had forgotten how the river opened the world and cooled it. All weariness dropped from him. For a long time he stood there. The currents came together in a long, murmuring wave.

Only a low wall of piled stone kept the spit across the channel from being an island of worn river rock and wet earth—acre enough to support the skinny trees and, where there wasn't bare rock, some tall grass. A good-sized syca-more had fallen into the water from the point of the island where the two streams met. It had been down a while, as most of its crown was broken off and gone, but the branches near its uprooted end still showed leaves, yellowing. Its white-gray trunk almost made a footlog to the island for Tobit. Almost. He liked thinking about a living bridge, one with wide leaves growing from it, like a shoot sprung from a stump.

He nodded once, then started looking for a way across the channel. On the far side of the island, the river seemed to pool and deepen without going fully slack. Demus might could stand up in the current there. It looked like water enough to bury and raise him.

A path through waist-deep grass ran up the bank to-ward the powerhouse. Tobit followed it along the channel and up the slope away from the river, then back down. It ended at the bottom of a flight of iron stairs going up to a grated catwalk that crossed the channel directly in front of the brick powerhouse. Below the walkway, the river boiled loudly where it surged up and out from under the mossy concrete base of the house. Holding the rails, Tobit crossed the narrow grate with care, like walking the ridge of a roof. The one time he looked up from his feet he saw the river through the scrim of trees. His first step down onto the island testified. This was the burying ground.

It wasn't precisely the old place, but it was old with spirit. It was where holiness had moved to. He felt it in the rock under the soft ground, heard it in the constant pour over the dam to his right. He saw the choir in their robes, lined up on two slabs of sandstone, their breath drawn in to break into song. Then the singers were gone. A fish hawk came down. He coasted on a sliding curve toward the slab with his claws open, then, at the last second before he touched, veered off downstream, all white underneath. With one stroke of his wings—Tobit heard the hush of them—he was gone over the trees the way Tobit had come.

He bent and untied his shoes, taking great care to keep his balance as he took them off one at a time. He removed his socks. For a long time, he looked across the river, witnessing the steady cascade over the dam, the ceaseless, changing wave the falling water made, the lightning-struck, woodpeckered pine on the far bank, the water as it divided then resealed itself among the piles and plains of rock, the glitter of broken glass in the weeds and gravel, the steady rowing of three blackbirds upstream and down and their lighting on reeds to look at him. His witnessing was not critical or questioning. His call was to see and accept.

A gust blew up the river, throwing a spat of spray on him and rustling the dry, dying leaves of the downed sycamore behind him. All the trees of the field shall clap their hands. He didn't study on it, only thought it—a bit of old scripture that laid a hand on the here and now where there wasn't anybody. Or maybe it was the here and now keeping touch with the old and gone. Tree has roots. He stepped in the water. Almost warm.

Tobit was not a shouter. The spirit left him alone that way. But he felt shouted into.

The way back here would be hard. Demus wouldn't see it, likely. He would say Tobit had just gone off and found a place on the river Demus could manage to walk to. Tobit couldn't help that. Let Demus see and accept for his ownself.

❧

Tobit didn't decide to leave the new burying ground. He couldn't have said when or how he put his shoes back on, his mind staying on Demus—not worrying, just dwelling. He simply came back to himself all at once, halfway back down the dirt road, and saw that the sun had stood straight up out of morning into afternoon. Everything changed all the time, in tiny ways, tiny shifts. It took a memory with pages as thin and crowded and orderly as Bible leaves for a body to see it, but see it you had to: if you didn't, you would miss what was under it that didn't change. The rock under the rock that rested on breath.

Nicodemus had missed it—had lived all his long life without that breath, though he had been a decent man when he wasn't mad or drinking. Demus's younger brother Ivery had been killed the same day the law let him go from jail, which was enough to turn anybody mean for these thirty years. Tobit had expected Demus to stay that way—to keep on fighting in the juke joints where he had once played the blues harp, to keep on drinking. Driving that block truck by himself for forty years.

Still, he wanted baptism. That was something. That was knowing you had built your house on the sand. It was also the reason Demus would want the old burying ground or nothing. Demus would think of the place the way he would of an ordinary grave. Demus wasn't like Ruby, who thought the dead were as present at their favorite fishing hole as they were in the graveyard. For Demus, everything had its one place—baptism no different from anything else. As if you could lock God up in a church.

Tobit remembered the redwings and was resting on them when the man in the truck pulled up beside him.

*You find it?* The liquor rode his breath all the way across the cab and out the passenger-side window.

*Yes sir, thank you.*

*Didn't take you long.*

*About as long as preaching.*

*Get in and I'll run you back.*

*I'm obliged, but I like to walk.*

*It's a ways, mister. Come on get in.*

*Thank you the same.*

*I know what you're thinking. Get in. I ain't like them others.*

*What others is that, sir?*

*The ones done whatever you come out here to find.*

*I come to find a old burying ground, sir.*

*Ain't no burying ground down that way. Not on the river. Flood'd tore it up if it was.*

*Burying like in baptizing, sir. Buried in the spirit, raised to walk in newness of life—that burying. That's my only business here.*

*Who you know buried down there?*

*Sir?*

*You looking for kin?*

*No, sir. My people is in Macon.*

*Come on. Get in. Let me run you back.*

*Thank you, sir. I like the walking. Somebody is coming for me directly.* Tobit raised a hand and started walking, slow, eyes down in an old way that he hadn't used in a long time but that was bitterly familiar. Behind him the truck sat idling. He could smell it burning oil. He took twenty steps before he heard it thunk into gear, then swing onto the highway headed back in the direction it had come from, moving neither fast nor slow as it passed him.

Still looking down at his feet, Tobit followed it with the corner of his eye. Once it topped the hill, he moved off the road and into the pines and scrub oaks, going deep enough into the woods to keep from being seen from the road. He hunkered into a squat behind a pine, watching the road through a gap in the trees until the truck came back, moving slowly. He heard it pull off and turn around at the road down to the river, heard the door squeak open.

*Preacher! You hear me? Preacher?!*

Tobit laid full down on the ground.

*Preacher! You come on out, now! You show me that burying!*

ॐ

Tobit missed evening preaching, too. It was almost moon-rise by the time he set foot on his porch. Inside, he poured pork and beans from a can into a pot on the stove and put some leftover ham in the frying pan. The ham had just start-ed to sizzle when there was a knock at his door.

Through the taped pane he saw the preacher, still in his tie, the single bulb of the porch light twinned in his glasses. Tobit turned the gas off and unlocked the door.

*Pastor.*

*We missed you today, brother T.*

*I missed being there.*

*You went looking for the grounds, I expect.*

*I did.* Tobit held the door open.

*Saw your dusty shoes out there on the stoop. I hope you found the place. Demus, he has taken a turn.*

*What sort of a turn?*

*Miss Myra thinks he's had a mini-stroke. Says he won't talk. Left side of his mouth is drooping down.*

*Well. When does he ever talk.*

The preacher took one of the two chairs at the table. *You found them, the old grounds?*

*Not the old grounds, no. But the spirit from them, I believe.*

*Then that's where we will take him.*

Tobit told him about the man in the truck. *Might be that we need to keep looking, pastor.*

*You said the spirit was there.*

*Look like the devil was, too.*

*Devil's always right there beside the spirit, brother T. Getting in the way.*

*That's the truth.*

*I wish you had not told him your business there.*

Tobit dipped beans onto two plates. He halved up the ham and laid the two pieces alongside the steaming beans and brought the plates to the table.

*I ought not to have said that, Tobit. You did God's work today. The Lord has not given us the spirit of fear but of love.*

They said grace in silence and ate. The preacher wouldn't accept the ham and made Tobit take it back. When they had finished, the preacher asked for Tobit's Bible. They prayed together over it, holding it between them, each man with one hand under it and the other on top of it. After the *amen*, the preacher opened it with his right hand: *There is a river that gladdens the city of God.* So they set it down that they would go.

Given Demus's condition, they could not wait for Sunday, the preacher said. Demus would be baptized Tuesday morning.

That night and the next morning, the preacher called the congregation. Most couldn't miss work. All promised to pray. The preacher came to the grocery store during Tobit's break. They sat at a folding table with cups of sugary burned coffee, the ache easing in Tobit's feet as soon as he sat down. The preacher asked Tobit whether they should call the law.

*The law'll tell us we can't do it.*

*Do we tell the brothers and sisters?*

Tobit sipped his coffee. *Ruby, she would bring her shot-gun.*

*She would. We would bring the devil with us.*

*He might just come on his own.*

*We will trust the spirit.*

*I hear you, pastor.*

*I better be going.* The pastor stood, pulling a rolled brown bag from his suit coat pocket. *I brought you some pound cake. Miss Myra thanks you for going out there yesterday.*

&

They met on the cinderblock steps of the church early the next morning, nine in all—more than Tobit had expected but still the smallest baptism group he could recall. There were three boys. Tobit knew two—Jourdain and DeCorby— only by having heard their names prayed. The third, Chava-rous, had preached and preached hard on Youth Sunday, wearing the same suit he had on today, which he couldn't quite fill yet. Then there was the pastor and Ruby and her niece Vida and the silent old deacon Bill. Everyone was in their Sunday best on Tuesday. Demus sat in Miss Ruby's Pontiac.

The pastor stood under the still burning streetlight and spoke in a quiet, carrying voice.

*I greet you in the name of the Lord. I am glad to see each and every one of you.* He named everyone there except Demus. *I thank those joining us through prayer this beautiful morning. They would be with us in body if they could. Their spirits are willing, but their bosses are weak.*

*We go today to where people don't know us. Our Lord is going with us. We are going to act in him, even if people out there act ugly to us, because we are about his business. That river is his, every drop and rock, same as the Jordan that baptized Jesus. We are strangers there, but we are also going where we are known—going where our new brother in Christ will know and be known.*

*Amen,* Ruby said. *This burying ground was ours a long time.*

*Miss Ruby is right as she can be. Brother Tobit, if you will now tell us the way.*

Tobit told them.

*Them ain't the grounds. Not by no mill.*

*The mill is closed, Ruby.*

*Brother Tobit's word is good enough for me,* the pastor said.

*Me, too,* said silent Bill.

*We broke the scripture on it. Psalm 46. There is a river that gladdens the city of God.*

*I saw the choir singing there,* Tobit said. *The old choir, from before Miss Myra's mama died.*

48

Ruby nodded at her feet through her thick glasses, then looked back up at the preacher, and that was the end of it.

*We are about to pray. Once we do, our new brother will be set apart. I will ask you to respect the spirit and the knowledge coming to him by keeping silent. If we get out there and he can't make his own way to water, you listen for that still, small voice, especially you boys there. The spirit will make a way.*

Then they prayed.

೭

Tobit rode in Ruby's car, sitting directly behind Demus, who was already dressed in his white robe. Demus's face was strangely softened, his eyes too clear, as if he had been emptied. The left corner of his mouth was seized up. As Tobit eased himself into the back seat, Ruby handed him a length of white cloth. Tobit passed it around Demus's forehead and knotted it in the back. Demus raised his right elbow, as if to ward off a blow.

The light grew around them as they drove, swallowing the last stars just before they passed through the village and crossed the bridge above the dam. Over the bridge rail, the river where it went over the dam was a straight, gun-blue edge against the mist downstream.

೭

Watching the other car growl over the gravel of the riverside lot, Tobit wished briefly for the baptisms of his childhood, when even people who owned cars walked or rode in wagons or on mules. All those being baptized had walked together. Once the birds began to sing again he felt better.

The others climbed out of the Chevrolet that the preacher had borrowed. The preacher was in his wine-colored robe now and so walked slower. He moved down the path through the arching brush toward the river, followed by Ruby, Vida, the boys, and Brother Bill, soundless in his soft zippered boots. As she passed under the branches, Ruby began to hum. Vida joined her. The procession wound slowly down the path, the walkers seven steps apart.

When they had disappeared into the woods, Tobit opened Demus's door and helped him climb out. Ruby and Vida's deep humming, fainter but still distinct against the constant gush of the tailrace, drew them down the path.

Demus's hand was shaky but his grip strong. On the trail he shook Tobit off, pausing only when he came to the iron stair up to the catwalk across the channel, where he let Tobit pass him. Tobit stayed a single tread ahead as they took the steps one at a time. At the top, the cold air rising from the pumphouse channel below bathed their hands and faces. Demus set off rapidly across the grating, his left foot dragging a little. Descending the steps on the far side, Demus missed the third rung from the bottom, falling against Tobit's back. Tobit had braced himself and stayed upright for both of them.

*Who is it holding me?*

Out of respect for the spirit, Tobit didn't answer. The boys gathered at the foot of the stairs, their fingers loose and ready. Jourdain had his knees bent as if he were about to run and catch a football. Tobit shook his head at them. This close to water, they were on holy ground. Tobit thought of King David's man who reached out to brace the Ark of the Covenant and was struck dead. God wouldn't do such as that to these boys, probably, but it was better to err on the side of fear. Let the spirit do the helping.

Demus crossed the marshy ground to the rock just fine, his left foot dragging a little. Vida stood where the water met the shore, the fallen sycamore behind her, singing the sun up. She drew the strength of that altar ground right up out of the earth and gave voice to it. Ruby, her left palm high and cocked back at the wrist, passed close by him, her white heels sinking in as she went, her old heartwood voice joining Vida's. The sun, rising upriver over the east bank, burned on the bone-gray upper branches and yellow leaves of the trees downriver and did not touch anyone yet. Tobit saw one star still quivering. In a broad pool downriver, a touch on the water sent a circle opening outward, then another. Another.

The boys, awkward, gravely humbled by their men's clothes, entered the song and gathered around Demus, falling into step with him across the uneven ground, not touching him even with their eyes. Tobit stood rooted to the gravel, feeling the air move over it and over the water. He let the boys take Demus. It seemed right to let the young be strong for him.

The preacher stood with his back to the river, three sticks of river cane held before him in his joined hands. He let Ruby and Vida arrive at the bend of their song and ebb down to a hum before he spoke.

*We gather here on this old Ocmulgee River that runs down to the ocean because we are called to. God has called us to this old place where things don't change, where the creation is still the creation, where the things of the Lord have kept on keeping on. We have come to thank the Lord for this river. To thank Him for his leading Brother Tobit to this burying ground. To thank Him for Jesus, buried and raised from the waters of the Jordan River before he was buried and raised from the tomb of rock.*

*You serpents in your holes in the bank, under your rocks, you tell your master he is losing another one to the Lord. You tell him the moving of these waters is about to carry an old life of sin away.*

The pastor stopped, though he had just found his rhythm. His eyes were on the treeline on the east bank where the sun was climbing. A wind came up, wafting leaves across the water.

*This is holy ground*, he said, and slipped his shoes off. He turned and waded in. With each stride the water rose further up his legs, darkening his robe and billowing it, drawing it downstream. Thigh-deep, he stopped and raised one of the canes high where all could see it.

*The Father!* He probed the river bottom, then sank the point of the cane into it so that it stood a hand's breadth above the surface. He moved three steps to the right, tapping a second stick like a blind man along the riverbed, then raised the cane high.

*The Son!* He sank the second stick to the right of the first.

*The Holy Ghost!* He sank the third to the left of the first one. He turned to face the baptismal party from within the arc the three canes made.

*Mothers of the church, bring the children forward.*

Ruby took Demus by the hand and led him the last few steps to the water's edge. Brother Bill knelt to tie two white leggings around the bottom of Demus's robe, but before he could, Demus walked in, looking off past the preacher. His white robe trapped a breeze as its hem grazed the surface. It swelled until Demus looked like a great, white-bundled baby. He was a sail. A bride. The loose ends of his headband fluttered. Then the current pushed the downstream edge of the gown into the air and Demus diminished to his usual hard, barbed-wire self.

The pastor took Demus's hands, as much to stop him walking all the way out into the river and probably across it as to follow the ritual. He folded the older man's hands in prayer and whispered words passed between them, many from the minister, two from Demus. The preacher put his right fist between Demus's hands and as Demus clenched his wrist the minister raised his left hand high.

*I baptize you brother in the name of the Father and the Son and the Holy Ghost.* He set his left hand between Demus's shoulder blades. The other hand the preacher pressed over Demus's mouth and nose, as Demus held on to the minister's wrist.

*Buried with him in baptism*—he lowered Demus backward into the current—*raised to walk in newness of life.* Just as the water closed over him, the preacher pulled Demus upright again.

Amens rose from the boys on the bank and from Brother Bill. Tobit heard his own voice, which didn't feel like his, joining them. Ruby let out a small shout. Vida sang, not loud:

*Wade—In the water*
*Wade—In the water, children*
*Wade—In the water*
*God's a going to trouble—the wa-ter.*

Ruby in her good hose met Demus and the preacher in the shallows, cupping Demus's face in her hands before she drew off his wet headscarf and flung it out into the current. Tobit watched it briefly, a thin white wreath, wheeling neither on nor under the surface but in it, being carried already toward a low falls at the bottom of the pool.

Tobit and Bill stepped into the river's edge, giving Demus the hand of fellowship. The boys and Vida, still singing, fell into the welcoming line as well. Hand by shaken hand, Demus was drawn up the line of brothers and sisters back onto the firm clay bank. Everyone stepped back into their shoes.

Ruby yanked the seam of Demus's robe: it opened with a chattering of snaps. So that was how she had finished it in time. Ruby caught Tobit's eye.

*You quit that grinning, old possum.* Tobit did not.

Vida's song eddied to a hum. The biggest towel Tobit had ever seen was cast around Demus's shoulders.

Ruby held the robe up by its shoulders, careful not to let it touch the ground. Vida, still humming, came to Ruby. As the youngest woman there, she stooped, took hold of the robe's hem at the corners and raised them, folding the cloth in half. Ruby took the corners. Again Vida folded the robe from the bottom. She held the left end, Ruby the right, and their hands met once more in a third and final fold. Bill stood ready with the leggings, which Ruby accepted and tied, one band crossing the other, around the robe. This bundle would be left in a sunny window in the church and turned regularly until it dried. It would serve as Demus's coffin pillow.

&#x264;

When Tobit went back to the cars for the thermos bottle of milky coffee and for Demus's dry clothes, he found the pickup truck driver from the road blocking the path, his brogans planted wide apart, his hands on his hips. He wore a hunting coat covered with a mottle of bark and leaves, a cap to match.

*You're on private property, preacher.*

*We'll be leaving, then.*

*You've done trespassed now.*

*Ain't no trespassing in the river, sir. The river ain't nobody's.*

*The land right up to it is somebody's. You got to have trespassed to have got to it. You got to trespass again to go home.*

*Get behind me, Satan.* It was the preacher, suddenly be-hind Tobit.

*He ain't Satan.*

*I ain't the devil himself, but I done his work.*

*You're mad at God, mister, not us. If you're mad at some-body, you don't take it out on their children. Ain't no satisfaction there.*

*God takes the sins of the father out on the child.*

*How's your boy?*

*Don't you talk about him.*

*I'm sent to talk about him.*

*Don't you talk.*

*You want us to pray for him? He messed up from that war?*

*Don't you talk.*

*We're in church right here and now, mister. That's why you're here, not meanness.*

*Here, now.* The preacher stepped around Tobit, his blue shirt-pocket New Testament leveled on the man, the spine of it held sideways between his thumb and first two fingers. *Come on and take this sword.*

Tobit took the little beat-up Bible, the page edges white where the silver had worn off, and held it out to the man.

*Take it. Go on.*

*You go to hell, preacher.*

*I'm already there, looking at you in the fire.*

It was like a rod running through the man's shoulders broke. He slumped, his empty hands hanging. His chin dropped into his chest so sharply the cap fell off his balding, spotted scalp.

Tobit took a step toward the man. He lowered the New Testament to where the man could see it.

*If you want it, you got to take it.*

*I can't.*

*Can't nobody do it for you.*

*I can't.*

*Worse than you has come. Meanest man I ever knew was just now baptized.*

*Worse than me ain't.*

*That's pride talking.*

*It's sin. It's blood.*

*Don't you tell me about blood. There's one blood washes out all the others.*

The man's body, starting with his shoulders, began to shake, as if with laughter.

*You quit that. Quit it.*

The man did not.

*We got a old man back yonder sick already and wet to the skin. Yes or no. This minute.*

The man hunched forward, burying his forehead in Tobit's shoulder. His hands closed on the Bible, one under and one over it.

*Quit it. Quit and stand up. Feel that strength.*

The man did. He lifted his wet eyes from Tobit's suit, looking him, then the preacher, in the face as if he had just waked up. *You said you'd pray for him.*

*What's your boy's name?*

*Joey. Joseph Mickry. He's missing.*

The preacher and Tobit prayed, each of them with a hand on one of the man's shoulders. After, he said he wanted to pray, too.

*All right.* Tobit bowed his head again.

*No. I can't like I am. I need to be washed. I need to be buried like your friend there.*

*No, sir. Prayer has to come before burying.*

The man looked at Tobit. *Bury me—please. This minute.*

*Mr. Mickry. You don't know what you're asking for.*

*Was you sent to tell me that, too?*

*Don't you mock the spirit. Don't you call on the lamb and then spit.*

The man slipped onto his knees. Tobit looked at the preacher. Ruby stood behind him, the boys and Bill at a distance behind her, watching.

*Pastor, counsel him.*

*Will you have me counsel you, Mr. Mickry?*

*No. I want him. He's my preacher.*

The preacher looked at Tobit, a strange smile on his face.

*He went to you-all's church,* Mickry said. *It was where he got called, he said.*

*Called!* Ruby bristled. *Called to go off and kill folks for wells of oil?! To make amends for your lynching!*

*I didn't lynch nobody.*

*I smell it all over you. If the call come to your boy in a church full of black folks, then that's why.*

*He was there with a girl. He—*

*He was there for the sins of his father. He was called to pay your bill, you devil. And you want baptizing!*

*You're right I'm a devil—but he ain't. He's a good boy. God wouldn't take it out on him.*

*He wouldn't? He would watch His own baby boy die on them sticks—His own perfect boy that didn't do nothing but feed folks and heal them—but you think He wouldn't write your soldier son's name on a quick bullet?*

*That's enough, Ruby. What God does is not for us to say. You remember the thief.*

*Don't you take me to the scripture, preacher.*

*And don't you sit on the judgment seat, sister.*

*I'm mother at this baptism. Demus is my child. Today is for him.*

*She's right. I deserve hell.*

*We all do.*

*But you 'specially.*

*Ruby! You stop, now.*

*You wouldn't say any of this in the church, Ruby.*

*If I didn't, somebody else would. The rocks would shout it out.*

*Come with me and Tobit, Ruby. Come on behind the cars and let's talk about this like the elders we ought to be.* They left Mickry there on his knees, Bill walking slowly toward him.

৵

The preacher leaned heavily against the bumper of the Chevrolet. Tobit said baptism wasn't theirs to deny. He said no one came to the altar clean. Ruby said Mickry hadn't come to Christ as all had to—he hadn't professed, so he couldn't be buried and raised. The preacher said that was true—that Mickry should come to church, walk the aisle, then be counseled (here he looked at Tobit for a long second), set apart, and provided for as any other new child of God would be.

Ruby stood with her feet apart and planted like a strong, rooted stump, her head bowed. After a time she opened her eyes and looked into Tobit's face, then the preacher's, void of joy.

*Paul was Saul until God struck him.*

*We agree, then? Let us pray in silence.* The preacher opened his hands. Tobit and Ruby each took one and joined their own hands as well. Ruby's grip was hot and hard as iron. They shared the darkness until the preacher's *amen* brought them back to the world.

Tobit remembered the thermos and fetched it, Ruby following him. She unlocked the trunk and drew out a big sweetgrass basket. Tobit took the coffee and bag of clothes from the front seat.

They found the preacher waiting where they had left Mickry.

*It appears he's gone.* A note of relief in his voice.

*His truck was still back there.*

*Mickry!*

*Calling him won't do any good.*

*He'll kill his fool self.*

*He'd have done that already was he going to.*

60

*He wanted baptizing first. He's got blood on him and he wanted that washed off.*

*We need to find him.*

*The children is who we need to find, Tobit.*

Ruby was right. Tobit and the preacher ran up the path. Slow as he was, Tobit still outran the pastor. He came out of the woods into the clearing where the trail bent up the hill, feeling eyes watching him. A wind gusted through, hollowing in his ears and shaking the dry grass. The hillside could have split open, the dead could have risen from it shaking dirt from their wounds and turned to face the sun, and Tobit would not have felt surprise. No one stood on the slope, nor was there any hiding place. Tobit took the steps two at a time.

Halfway across the narrow iron bridge, the wind caught Tobit from behind, almost toppling him as it blew across the channel and rocked the sycamores on the island, stripping leaves in a fluttering cloud from the branches and revealing the whole river like a shard of mirror in the full morning sun. Holding still to see between the bars of the trees, Tobit watched Chavarous, waist-deep, raising a pink-faced, white-shirted figure from the moving water. The shape in the soaked shirt sagged onto its knees. Tobit stayed where he was, not wanting to be any closer, so he was still watching when Demus appeared from nowhere, tottering through the current to place both hands on the stooped figure's crown as if to bless it. The left hand slid off. Then the right one found the strength to push the balding head back under and hold it there.

Tobit started forward, but something had a grip on him, too. He heard Ruby say *You wait on the Lord. Wait and see.* The words seemed to come to Tobit across a great distance.

Demus did not let up, though Jourdain and DeCorby ran over the water toward him, wind flapping in their clothes. The man in the water did not thrash or struggle. He let himself be held under. He was quiet at last. He stayed that way, even as the hands of the boys easily drew Demus away—Demus who seemed suddenly as light as the leaves that descended, flaring yellow, around them. The boys' hands lifted the man in his sopping shirttail back into the terrible air. They stood him on his feet, though it seemed the river at any moment might carry him—might carry all of them—away.

# Seven Islands

## I.

In the grip of the river, Rea forgot her nine-months-dead dad, the failing pawn shop he had left her, and the new pain in the old scar where her left breast had once been—the dull throb like a heart that beat five times a week. The missed payments on the pawn shop sank, and with them the failed attempts to think up ways to stock the shelves and cases without enough cash to pay out on the used generators, mature guitars, and guns that people would pay good money for.

Halfway through the Seven Islands, Rea knew from the sustained roar downstream that she should beach the kayak among the blunt boulders at the head of the small mid-river isle, then wind her way through the thicket of sweetgums and undergrowth to the other end where the rock reached out above the rapid—a perfect place to scout the drops—but she couldn't summon a sense of threat. The kayak, a battered, plastic, flatwater boat, had a long, new furrow from where Rea had shoved it under the chain link around the back of the pawn shop after the deputies had padlocked the doors. Wounded, the boat seemed to want to plunge on, like a dog fighting a leash. With clouds starting to darken the sky upstream, she let the river have her. The taut horizon line the shoal made across the river felt like the edge Rea had been waiting to toe.

She went straight into the first drop, every tendon in her arms and shoulders working to keep the kayak in the flow, which met and accepted her as long as she matched its pace. The river drew her into the lee of the island where, left paddle blade still in the water, she could catch her breath for the fast water coming up. The last time she had floated this eddy, she had found herself face to face with a young, weasely-looking river otter crouched on a rock. The animal had been gone in the half-second it took to realize she was seeing it. That was the river: giving with one hand as it took away with the other. Seeing the otter—there, then gone, like the antique coins her father used to make vanish when customers brought them in to sell—Rea had known better than to expect to find another one, but she had hoped.

The current stiffened, pushing Rea toward a line of rock that cut straight across the river from the right bank to the isle. She muscled the boat right through the one gap, going almost fully broadside to the current to shoot through it at the necessary slant. She planted the paddle to the left side of the boat and leaned back on it to push left, parallel to a second channel-spanning ledge. The kayak yawed sideways through the headlong froth until her bow met a spill surging around the rocky tail of the island. The fast water and the four drops coming up filled her attention. She lost what she wanted to lose.

The same moment, she found a child where no child should be.

The kid stood with his side to her on a hump of granite above the drop she had just come down. The river around him bulged with stone and blew itself into a lather through the stair-step maze of islets. A PFD, man-sized and so loose it almost didn't matter that it wasn't buckled, hung to the kid's knees. The child's bare left foot was glaringly pale against the moss on the rock. The riddle of how the boy— was it a short-haired girl?—came to be there dissolved in a buzz of alarm as Rea realized the drop-off behind the kid's rock was twice his height. Two steps in any direction and the kid would either be swept down the rapid Rea was about to run or would fall onto the toothy jumble of rock over the shoal edge. The standing waves weren't more than hip-deep on an adult, but the force of the current under them would make standing upright impossible.

All of this penetrated Rea in a single second. At that second's end, the boy—it was a boy, yes—turned and saw her.

∾

Rea tried to back-paddle, but the liquid gravity of the current had already seized her, pushing her toward a chute between boulders that was narrower than the boat. She was in and of it, now, as she had wanted to be from the time the foreclosure warning had come. Her only way was through.

From the corner of her eye, she saw the boy bend his knees as if to jump off his island toward her.

*No!* Rea shouted. *Sit down!*

The boy started backward, stung.

*It's okay!* Rea yelled, trying to soften the words. *I'll stop down below, buddy.*

Distracted, Rea lost her track, went too far left, and was missing the chute and headed for a sandstone undercut that was liable to catch her bow and wedge her against the current.

Rea put all her weight into getting back on her original line into the chute of the first waterfall, her soles hard against the foot pegs, her legs braced against the inside gunwales, all of her a lever. The bow yawed sluggishly back toward the blur of water breaking over the lip of the falls, but Rea could feel that she was moving too slowly. Taking the drop off-pace, her tail would be swept left into the undercut ledge she had just barely missed with her bow. Broadside to the current, she would either swamp or flip.

The chute sucked her in. With room for one more big stroke before the rocks on either side closed her in, Rea put her hips and back into it, shooting herself through the notch, then bracing to cut back to the right, the standing wave throwing two gallons of cold river water over the edge of the too-big cockpit.

The second drop, alongside a round boulder big as a VW, plunged into a souse hole that wanted to keep and play with everything that floated. Whatever went over that spill would plunge halfway to the bottom, come up, then be driven down again in a circular drowning dance that would go on as long as water and rock kept up their argument. Back up to river speed, ready and on her line this time, she beat the hole easily. The same was true of the last two, though the final one banged up the boat. The water Rea had taken on from the wave below the first drop made her grind on the slanting sandstone table barely covered by the standing waves at the shoal's bottom. She winced.

Rea breathed deeper. She let the river bump her gently onto a low swell of mossy stone, then scanned the upstream horizon line for the boy. There he was, not sitting, but squatting with his knees together and held to his chest inside the life jacket, looking downstream like an odd idol at Rea. She expected to see someone else nearby—a dad with a spinning rod, a ten-pocket Orvis vest, a hat prickling with woolly buggers, or maybe an uncle or an older brother just upstream bailing a canoe.

Rea saw no one.

*Hey*, she called. *Can you hear me?*

The boy didn't move. Rea shouted louder. The boy's blond mop of a head came up, but he did not shout back. He raised his hands to shade his eyes as he looked at her.

There was nothing else to do but go back to him. Rea stuffed a length of cord and her bottle of water into one pocket of her PFD and her lunch in its small vinyl dry bag into the other. Five steps into the river, off balance on the rocks, she already needed both hands to stay upright in the current. Rock by rock, she picked out a mostly dry route to climb the shoal back up to the boy. She had to go up the middle of the riverbed toward the left bank, ending at a point upstream of the boy. From there she rock-hopped down to his hump of granite, crossing half the width of the river to get to him.

It was a slick, uneven, rock-rolling treachery of a trip. On the way, Rea checked the banks and mid-river rocks continually for the boy's grown-ups. The boy didn't look around at all, only watched Rea coming, still in his squat. Worry began to swirl in Rea's gut.

Covering seventy yards took nearly twenty minutes. Finally Rea came abreast of the boy's rock. She slipped over the long sandstone ridge she had paddled parallel to earlier and lowered herself into the river on the other side, letting it carry her toward the kid, her hand brushing along the rock, her old torn-up river sneakers pointed downstream. When the ridge dived under the surface, Rea dragged herself up on its last slippery knuckle and looked across the waterfall at the kid, maybe a dozen feet away now, the current between them fast and deep.

He still watched her intently. His arms were red, as was the shoeless foot that had looked so pale a little while ago. There was a thumb-sized blister above his right elbow.

*You all right?*

The boy nodded.

*Can you tell me who you're with? Is your dad out here?*

The boy shook his head vigorously.

*You're not by yourself, are you?*

Nothing—not a nod or a headshake. Stillness. Rea thought she saw tears being held back fiercely.

*How did you get out here? Can you tell me?*

Again the boy shook his head.

*I'm Rea.*

A wave—quick.

*You got a name, buddy?*

Again nothing.

*Br'er Rabbit? Scooby Doo?*

The corners of his mouth didn't move. His eyes were huge, dark, and fixed on Rea's face.

*Think I can guess it?*

A headshake. The boy's clothes looked dry.

*No? Well, anyway—I'm a friend, buddy. Where's your folks?*

The boy let go of his knees, his hands half open out in front of him as if he were about to clap a mosquito. He held them there like that, as if there were something between them only he could see. Then he looked again at Rea.

*I don't get that, buddy.*

The kid couldn't talk—or wouldn't. Rea again scanned the banks. They sloped too steeply down to the water for portaging, and the woods, all of it Oconee National Forest land, were thick, the trees close together. They were eight miles from the nearest shack. It had taken the boy's sawed-off dungarees a while to dry out. That sunburn had taken a while to get, too.

*You hungry, Scooby? Thirsty?* Rea worked the bottle of water and the lunch out of her vest. *Don't you miss this, now, you hear?*

He caught both, immediately draining the water bottle, then wolfing Rea's peanut butter and banana sandwich. Rea had never seen anyone eat that much peanut butter without drinking along the way to wash it down, and she said so.

As he ate, she scanned the banks and the island upstream of them. This was the most visible place on the river. It made sense to stay put until someone showed up to claim him. Whoever it was, they would have to come soon. Upriver, the clouds were dark as a bruise. An early fall storm was brewing.

They sat there looking across the flow at each other for a while. Upstream of them near the prow of the island a bird floated across the sky. Rea squinted at it and spoke calmly to the boy.

*Osprey. Circling. He's hunting for a fish. One time not far from here I seen an osprey drop a fish from way high up and another osprey caught it. You believe that? They say that's how they court. The male drops it and then the female, if she likes the look of him, she catches it. I'm not sure I believe it, myself. I've only seen it that one time.*

Rea's father's years of reading about the river had leaked out of him in the pawn shop—Hernando de Soto, Brimms, Bartram, the Yuchi, Hitchiti, and other Muscogees, the skin trade, ferries and cotton mills, murderers hiding out on wooded islands, the Union slaughtering dozens of exhausted mules on river islands to keep them out of Confederate hands, the building of the big power-generating dam to fill Jackson Lake and of the small, low-head one down at Juliette. When she was a girl, he had told these stories on slow summer afternoons to the changing gaggle of old men who loitered in the shop for the free air conditioning. Odis talked only when his hands were busy cleaning an old coin or sorting through one of the boxes of books or papers he bought for a few dollars at country auctions. He knew exactly how much patina to leave on the coins to enhance the value, knew which ones not to clean at all. Rea had been reminded of this when she cashed out the coins, his specialty, to a single internet buyer, accepting maybe two-thirds of their worth and probably twice what her dad had paid for them.

*An osprey was big medicine to the Muscogee. They have that forked eye that sees in all three worlds—the sky, the land and water, and the underworld. They're awake to all three.*

The baskets and coffee cans of Indian scrapers, points, and potsherds people had tried to sell also got her father going. He would finger every edge, never buying any of it for fear of robbing a grave. Rea had read some of Odis's books herself. Some of them her father had read aloud in the shop, to his coffee-sipping cronies and to Koenig, the cop who came in with lists of stolen guns, jewelry, and tools for Odis to be on the lookout for. Her father's voice and the voice under the words in the books roiled together in her memory. He had never bought anything hot that she knew of, though every month or so he would point out an amp or a Ruger on Koenig's list that he had seen and turned down. Odis also never called the cops when some shiftless bastard tried to fence a set of silver or a strand of pearls, which was why Koenig kept coming by.

To unclench the boy, maybe get him talking, Rea told him what her father had told her.

*An osprey eye can see a gnat on a reed. They're some kind of strong, some kind of fierce. You don't want to be on the wrong end of that hooked beak. Don't you worry. You're too big for him. Not that he's scared of you, now. He's careful. Scared and careful, those are two different things.*

Rea told him that de Soto's priests had baptized a couple of Yuchi or Hitchiti boys somewhere on this river—the boys had asked for the sacrament and the friars traveling with de Soto had granted it to them by immersing them and christening them John and Mark. As a girl, Rea had liked the sound of *New World*. She had also liked the fact that the story had kids in it—and she had liked the sound of *christen*, a verb she had never heard until her father read it aloud. It rhymed with *glisten*, which made Rea think the boys weren't just being named, but lit up somehow. The story sort of went with her dad's description of native cradleboards being left beside rapids by mothers so the babies could listen to the river's teaching. John and Mark were baptized both ways— steeped in wildness and rebellion on the one hand, then washed clean of it on the other. In another version of the baptism story—one that Rea dismissed as soon as she heard it—the boys weren't boys but chieftains. Crossing the 83 bridge one day in her father's old Dodge, Rea had asked him where the baptism happened. She had been looking out the window at the time, expecting to see a round rock nest in the river somewhere—a bowl for baptizing. No one knew for sure, he had said, but probably near Macon.

The boy looked at the water as she talked, not at her, but she could tell he listened. Whatever else he might be, he wasn't deaf.

❧

*All right, buddy. You see those clouds back there? There's thunder and lightning in them. I've got to beat those to the bridge.* There was still no sign of his people and the sky had grown two shades darker since she had reached him. Rea stood up. *Lightning on a river ain't nothing to laugh at.*

The boy looked at Rea's rock where the river lapped it.

*I don't want to leave you here, but I'm not taking you unless you want to go. You seem like a good kid, but you're not my kin and there's nobody to decide for you. You have to do it.*

The boy looked her in the face. He took a half step toward her, his toe in the water.

*All right, then. Here I come. Stand up and get ready to catch a line.*

❧

Rea rock-hopped upstream, slid down into the pool where the current was calmer, and let the river carry her feet-first in her PFD toward the boy's rock, a coil of paracord in her hand. Once she floated into range, she tossed the boy one end of it and held on to the other.

*Pull me in.*

The boy knew how to pull a rope. He leaned back, dragged her hand over hand until Rea felt bottom and el-

73

bowed up onto the kid's island. She told the boy the water felt good.

*You ready?* Rea asked. The boy held very still.

One of the boy's hands fluttered, stopped.

*What is that—you signing? Can't you talk?*

The boy stared past her across the rocks, his mouth a hard line.

*Fine, then. People talk too much anyway. Here, let's trade vests. You'll have to float some to get down to the boat.*

The boy looked at her darkly.

*We'll trade back. No way I'm letting you keep my lucky life jacket.* Rea took off her PFD to zip and buckle it on the boy, tugging the side straps as tight as they would go. The boy's cheap vest—three chunks of foam in faded, threadbare nylon with no zipper and only one buckle left—hung almost as big on Rea as it had on him.

Together they climbed, slid, and waded down the shoal, staying out of the holes and drops and keeping to the margins of the flow. Rea tied one end of the cord to the loop on the boy's back and the other to her own PFD. The first pool, hip-deep on Rea, seemed to wake the kid up. He ducked his head in and paddled.

*Don't kick,* Rea told him. *A rock'll break your ankle. Paddle your hands all you want. Look where you're going.*

Going down the shoals took a third the time climbing up had. When they came to the kayak, the boy stepped into the cockpit. For the first time, the boat felt like hers.

*Okay,* Rea said. *Good. But you have to let me get in first.*

## II.

Rea and the boy were a tight fit until Rea unbuckled her borrowed, bulky PFD. As she loosened the lower strap the right pocket rapped her knuckles. Her palm flattened through the nylon against a hard, heavy curve. She sat the boy in front of her, inside the open halves of the worn-out life jacket she still wore, then told him to stay centered and keep his legs down inside the boat, to sit up straight and be careful of the paddle. She pushed off. The river nosed their bow around toward the open channel below the shoals. Thunder rolled distantly upstream. With one hand on the paddle across the cockpit forward of the boy, she carefully slipped the other into the PFD pocket and confirmed it: what she had felt was a pistol.

It was a derringer, a little badass chrome comma of a gun—scarred, one grip cracked, easy to hide in her fist. A steady stream of these had passed through the long glass case in the shop, most of them not pawns but outright sales by women who had received them from husbands or fathers and who seemed more afraid of the guns than of the criminals they were supposed to deter. It was often women who bought them, too. They had stocked a few with pink grips, even. Near the end, when the brain tumor was making him obsessive, her father had gotten it in his head that Rea needed one, that she wasn't safe. It had been funny almost, how he cared at the end when he hadn't cared at all during his drinking years. Rea felt the same way about the pawn shop, only caring about it when it became clear she would lose it.

Thinking about the shop, she remembered the pegboard along one wall, her job of hanging belt- and shoulder-holsters on the rows of rubber-tipped prongs as her father talked.

꙰

*Those people I was telling you about before, the first folks, they had boats carved out of huge cypress and poplar trees, some of them sixty feet long. They traded down the river in them for shells that they would carve and make beads from. They didn't run these shoals, probably, not in those heavy dugouts. Up here they had a trading path, a regular road that crossed the river up around the Seven Islands and went all through Alabama, Mississippi, Texas—maybe all the way down to Mexico, where they say they came from, way back. Along in here they would either get on the river, below that last big rapid where I met you, and float down to the coast, or turn west. Folks went up and down that path all the time, wore it into a trench. Strangers came through on it, too. They took care, dealing with strangers. A stranger, he can be God or the devil either one. There were stab-fingers back then that looked and talked like people, but their pointer finger was sharp and hard as a tooth. Stabfingers could sound just like somebody you knew, then, once you let your guard down, they'd grow that stone finger out in a flash right through your heart.*

*Up at the bluffs where the dam is now, there was another monster the people steered clear of. There was a cave in the hill there, where a water-panther lived—a big snake with wings and claws and the head of a cougar. They stayed away from*

76

*there. That's saying a lot. Those first people, they weren't afraid of much. They ended up chasing the Spanish down the Mississippi and out of the country with their dugouts, sixty, seventy warriors to a boat.*

&

The beginning of the end came when Rea had to sell the coins that were the capital core of the shop, the endowment. Three payments later, when she had been short again, she had to face facts. Losing Odis Loan & Pawn wouldn't kill her. She had never loved it—even hated it when she was in foster care and later, after high school, when she had to cover for her father during his benders. Still, she had felt grief. His place at the counter, his swiveling stool, the stacks of paper in the back office, his loupe. His place in the shop she was certain of, if not his place in her. Her love for him was laced with rage—a scarred, doubled-up love, intensified by the fact that he had come back to her from the bottle.

They paddled through what was left of the old mill—a broken stone wall on the right bank and just downstream of it a square room, its roof gone so long ago it was crowded with foot-thick trees. The boy looked through a window with no frame or sash at the grove penned up in stone. Rea's father had told her that an old man, no good for much else in the mill, had sat at that window, making sure nothing obstructed the intake or damaged the sluice that once ran down the riverbank upstream, diverting water to boilers that forced steam into the turbines that drove the cotton looms. What her father Odis had told Rea, Rea told the boy.

*The old watcher's job was a good one—far enough from the looms that they didn't drown out your thinking.* The boy stared as they passed the room, turning to watch it dissolve into the trees.

*You hear that quiet? When I was a girl we lived beside a mill. It hummed all day and all night. You could put your hand on the brick wall of it and that sound would vibrate right through your arm and into your teeth. My mama worked there for a while.*

Her father had a cool head for the pawn business, tempered by a conviction that he was a working person's last resort. For a few years in the late '80s he had rented tools out of the shop, letting out for a half-day's fee ladders, wrench sets, floor nailers, and floats and trowels. He called them blood tools. He would apply a portion of the rent to the loan, which let a few roofers, masons, and painters limp back into business one job at a time. Odis—Rea had started calling her father Odis then, when saying *Daddy* made her too angry—had known when he was buying tools from someone who knew their use and who had worn them into a form better than new.

The sun lit a swath ahead of them and presently they reached it. The river narrowed, lacing itself in shallow channels between small islands of rock and very fine orange sand. The boy watched the blurred coble of the bottom passing. Rea stopped paddling in the straightaway below where Wise Creek entered the river from the left, cooling it.

*Turtles, they like this stretch. Watch up ahead of us on top of rocks and stick-ups. They look like a crooked line of pies.*

As Rea said it there was a loud plop along the right bank at two o'clock ahead of them. Rea looked over in time to see the veiny, green-and-yellow mottle of turtles clawing off a log. They flashed and vanished in the clear water.

*Look at their ears.*

The boy spotted two lying on a rock nearly mid-river. Rea followed the boy's eye to them.

*Their heads will come up in a second.* Rea gently put her hand into the PFD pocket for the pistol.

The turtle nearest them craned its neck. The boy leaned forward.

Rea thumbed down the barrel lever, breaching it open so that the brass butts of the twin .38 bullets gleamed in the sunlight. She quickly closed it, pushed the lever back to lock, and re-pocketed the pistol.

*See that color? Red-eared slider.* Rea resumed paddling. *I bet you can see why they call them sliders.*

The boy nodded. Both turtles teetered into the river.

*They don't need ears for you, now, do they?*

The boy turned and looked up at Rea, his mouth slightly open as if he were about to say something. His smile flickered and was gone, quick as the turtles once they hit the water.

∾

*What the Spanish didn't know about this country saved them. De Soto's army would never have survived except for two things—horses and ignorance. They were what made the Spanish look invincible. The natives had never seen a horse before de So-*

to's cavalry showed up, and they had never seen people traipse right through places filled with demons and live through it. They were impressed. De Soto had dogs, too—big, mean wolfhounds, trained to run people down and tear them apart.

They called him the son of the sun, and he played that up. When he attacked villages, he did it at dawn. He'd give Son-of-the-Sun as his name through his translators. Probably no Indian mistook de Soto for God. He couldn't speak their language without a slave to translate, he didn't know where he was going, he was easy to fool. They knew he was no god, but they had the sense not to contradict him. They figured out pretty quick what he wanted, which was gold, and they always said yes, there's gold, just not here. Then they pointed him toward the territory of their enemies or at least the chiefdoms of strangers. They usually cooked up a pretty good story to go with the vague directions, too. And some head men sent him through places where they thought no one could survive—places where water-panthers lived or where there was nothing to eat, where only a complete fool would go. They survived those places, so they seemed protected. The natives knew the Spanish were human by the way they ate, fought, went after women, and got sick. Before de Soto broke his first winter camp down in Florida, the Guales there had already figured out how to get cane arrows through Spanish chainmail. They took the points off, so the cane would splinter through the little rings. It took a while for de Soto to lose, but he lost. Everybody that greedy bastard met did, too. He's dead in the Mississippi mud to this day.

## III.

In the last two s-bends upstream of the take-out at the bridge, Rea pulled them up in an eddy along a low rock shelf on the left bank. She needed time to think through what she should do at the take-out, so she decided to pull off and get out. She figured one of three things could happen at the bridge. One, she would find a distraught, panic-ragged set of parents with a ranger staring upriver waiting for them. Two, she would finally find what she had half expected all day—a bridge piling or a strainer tree with a body or boat snarled up in it. Three—this she feared most—she would find nothing.

The boy clambered out as soon as Rea laid a hand on the rock to stop them. They would have flipped had the water not been so shallow. He set off up the steep sandy bank at a run.

*Hey*, Rea said, surprised. He turned to look back at her, his knees pressed together.

*Oh. I'm sorry, buddy.* The boy had drained the water bottle an hour ago. *Can you go with the vest on?*

The boy shook his head quickly.

*You better undo it, then. Go on, like I showed you.*

The boy pressed at the buckle, beginning to dance.

*Just a minute.* Rea climbed out of the kayak and up the bank to unsnap the vest.

The boy ducked behind a big sycamore over the crest of the bank. Rea shrugged into her vest, moving the derringer from the pocket of the kid's too-big PFD into her own.

The boy was halfway back down the bank when she heard the outboard motor.

Downstream, a silver johnboat cruised against the current along the middle of the river. Rea could just see it between the branches of a tree fallen at the point of the bend. It moved at quarter speed, the outboard muttering. Someone checking limb lines—or looking for something.

Rea turned to the boy. He was scrambling back up the slope.

*Buddy? Wait, kiddo. I need you.* Rea hoofed up after him, finding the boy curled behind the base of the sycamore, his head hunched down. Their eyes met. The boy shook his head.

*Tell me, little man.* But the boy only shook his head as if he would never stop.

Rea turned back toward the river, taking a step, then sliding on her heels down the crumbling sandy clay of the bank to the kayak. She lifted the paddle and poked the worn-out PFD out of sight in the cockpit just as the boat hove around the bend.

A tan face in shooting glasses with amber lenses below a Titleist golf cap swung from the opposite bank to the channel ahead, then to Rea. Rea nodded. The boat throttled down to idle. The man in the cap nodded back.

*Hidy. You seen a boy?* The man stood and held a hand at waist level. *About so tall?*

Rea looked at the hand, then saw past it to the man's jeans pocket—the black grip of a small automatic pistol sticking out of it just below his turquoise-tooled belt.

*You lose one? How old is he?*

*Oh, he's little. About that tall.* The hand again. His heavy canvas work jeans hadn't ever been worked in. *I didn't lose him. He's a thief.*

*Is that so?*

*He stole the catalytic convertors out of two of my pickups. Snuck up from the river. Stole a canoe, too.*

*A kid that little?*

*Last night. He had help, I 'magine. Can't see much on the video except that he's a kid.*

*Where was this?*

*My river place, a couple miles below the dam. It's fenced and gated. He had to have come up from the river.*

*You let the rangers know?*

*They're looking, too. Ought to be using their helicopter.*

*When did they get a helicopter?*

*You know they got one, the DNR. Paid for with our taxes.*

*Here*—Rea grabbed the cockpit of the kayak and began to drag it sideways all the way out of the river onto the rock and clay shore—*I'll ride with you, help you look.*

*I don't want to put you out.* Rea saw in the way he leaned toward her his realization that he was talking to a female. *I got a couple of fellows up at the shoals looking, coming my way.* He sat back down. *Is that your truck up at the bridge? That Toyota?*

Rea nodded.

*It looked all right, but if I was you, ma'am, I'd get on down to it.* He flipped the lever on the side of the motor out of neutral. *We'll find him, You stay safe, now.*

83

On the word *safe* he twisted the grip on the outboard and plowed full speed up the river, his free hand raised in a curt way. He was gone.

Rea made a show of getting in the boat and pushing off, thinking she would go as far as the take-out, then paddle back if it was clear.

The boy wouldn't let her. He was leaping down the bank, heedless. He didn't stop at the water's edge but ran straight in, splashing. Rea looked upriver, down, scanned the banks. She held up a palm toward the boy, who stopped. Rea spoke low.

*Wasn't nobody leaving you, buddy. That peckerwood you're so scared of, he might have left somebody behind him to watch the river. I needed to see if he did, that was all.*

The boy stared at the nose of the kayak, his mouth set in that hard line Rea was getting to know well.

*You talk, boy. Tell me right now.*

The boy stood still as a statue.

*Who was that in the boat? You know him? Did you steal from him?*

He shook his head.

*Were you with somebody that did? You running away? Which one you shaking me off about—running away?* The boy nodded.

*Were you with somebody? Okay. Did they leave you? This morning? All right. All right. You about to cry? Good, 'cause sound carries out here.*

Rea pulled the boy's PFD out of the kayak's bow, paddled far enough out to where the current would carry it past the point, then let it go. She watched it float away, then paddled back to the boy.

*Take off your shirt,* she told him, keeping her voice low. The boy did, dragging it up over his head. Rea had intended to drop the shirt in for the Titleist to find later—a false trail. A sooty bruise clouded the left side of his stomach where his ribs showed. Rea saw two red circles above the boy's cutoffs.

*Never mind, buddy. Leave it on.*

From where Rea floated, she could see the river-left end of the bridge. No one was on it that she could see. Downstream, the life jacket, spread open on the water, turned lazily in the current.

*You're not going to like this, buddy,* she said. *I got to leave you for a little while. I'm coming back to get you, but I got to leave you. You go up that bank again and walk straight away from the river a hundred yards or so. There's a trail there. You turn right on it and follow it, and it'll take you to a dirt road that goes down to the bridge where my truck is. It's not far. Don't come out on the road when you see it. You stay down the trail. Get where nobody can see you but you can see the road. I'll be in a little black pickup truck. You come get in quick as you can when you see me stop. You got it?*

Rea expected the boy to resist—maybe to tear up again—but he only turned immediately and started back through the water for the bank. When he reached it, Rea saw his feet. Both were bare now.

*Wait.* Rea pulled off her wet canvas high-tops and threw the sneakers one at a time to the boy. *Can you tie shoes? Good. Get them on quick, now. Hey.*

The boy turned at the crest of the bank.

*You wait as long as you have to. I'll come.*

Rea let the current carry her down, hugging the left bank. She gave the life jacket time to float down well ahead of her. Once around the point, she kept in its eddy, watching the overgrown banks. Light again, the kayak wanted to trot. She had to hold it back.

Nothing moved ahead. A rope with a broom handle tied to its end hung down from a sycamore leaning off the river-right bank. On a Saturday or Sunday teenagers in cut-offs and bikini tops would have been all over it, whooping. A grannie with a tall boy would have been sitting in a lawn chair up to her waist in the river. Rea had never cared much for such folk, the way they asked how many she had caught and where she had put in, the way they left their butts, cans, and underwear in the shallows and along the banks. Rea had been happy it was a weekday when she put in because she knew she wouldn't see such people. Now she wished for them.

She was hugging the bank almost within casting distance of the mud boat ramp on the left shore when she heard someone slosh rapidly into the water. Through a screen of low-hanging branches, she watched a teenaged boy, wiry and tall, focused on something in the middle of the channel and plowing hip-deep towards it. He wore a white tank undershirt, sagging baggy shorts, and a baseball cap with a flattened brim. He was the dropout she had seen across the pawn shop counter a hundred times, minus the car stereo or the box of CDs or the electrician's tools they

86

wanted top dollar for. He even had the gold choker around his neck. Rea floated into plain view along the bank, but the teen didn't see her.

The boy-man, his back to Rea, leaned, reaching until he almost dipped his weak, wispy beard down into the water. He came upright with the boy's worn-out PFD, raising and eyeing it like a dripping stringer of catfish. The teenager was still looking at it, turning it in his hands, when Rea stuck her paddle blade in and pushed for the foot of the ramp. She saw already that the mud there was thoroughly tracked by lug-sole boot prints and at least two different kinds of sneakers.

*Hey, man. This yours?*

Rea turned. *Hey.* She patted her vest twice. *Nah.*

*You see anybody up yonder?*

*Guy in a johnboat, looking for a kid. That's not his jacket, is it—the kid's?*

*Oh, no. This here is a man's. Way too big for him.*

*That's good news, then. You all want help finding him?*

*Thanks, but no. It's a bunch of us up there at the shoals.*

*Crazy kid, dragging a catalytic to the river.*

*You got that right.*

*There's some sorry people in this world.* Rea wanted to learn more, but not at the risk of making herself memorable. She chinned the boat onto the mud of the ramp and climbed out.

Under the bridge there was only her beat-up Toyota. She backed it down the ramp, seeing in her rearview mirror the teenager standing by the kayak, looking into the cockpit.

Rea got out. As she walked toward him the boy bent and reached into the boat. Rea had put the paddle in the truck bed before backing it down the slope. She reached over and lifted it, unclicking it at its middle and getting a double-fisted grip on one of the two halves as if it were an axe. The thrifty aluminum was too light by far. She looked at the back of his head, visualizing the line running from ear to ear where she would have to hit him.

*You got one nice seat in that mother.*

*Yeah.* Rea cocked the half-paddle back like a baseball bat, then saw the teen's eyes were already back on the river. *I bet you can paddle that baby all day long and not even feel it.*

Rea had one leg in the truck when the teenager said *Hey.* He was suddenly there facing her through the open door. There was a slight cast in one of his eyes—the right one angled off on its own.

*I'm sorry about calling you sir.*

*I get that a lot. Ought to grow my hair out.*

*Don't see all that many ladies out here. No offense.*

*None taken. Hope you find him.*

He was already loping back down to the river.

❧

When Rea slewed to a stop, the boy came immediately out of the woods. Rea had him lie down in the floorboard with her PFD and towel over him. She warned the kid it would be a rough ride out to the road, and it was. They bounced over the rugged forest service crush-and-run road, taking the long, backdoor way out to avoid the Highway 83 bridge. In a few miles the two-rut track ran along the river, roller-coastering along the waist of a ridge above it. Rea drove faster than she usually did along this stretch. Anybody hiding in the trees would think twice before he jumped out into the road.

Down the hill from the old primitive Baptist church, two turkeys strutted across the clay ahead of them. The second stopped halfway, eyeing the truck from one side of its head. Rea slid to a stop.

*Hey, buddy. Get up and look.*

The boy did. He and the tom appraised each other coolly.

*If I had a shotgun anywhere in here you never would of seen them. Brain like a BB, but smart as hell where their skin's concerned.*

Everything Rea wasn't—but the right luck could be better than brains, and luck had parked Tabby's green Department of Natural Resources pickup just off the road behind the church. Rea felt the boy tense up as he saw it.

*Don't panic. I know what I'm doing.* Rea pulled in behind the other truck, told the boy to sit tight, and got out.

## IV.

Tabby had the brown ball cap and sunglasses on. Something was up. She didn't smile.

*Hey, Rea. That was one slow paddle.*

*Hey, Tabby. I got hung up. I got to ask you something.*

*All right. So ask.*

89

*It's not official, see. I'm not asking the DNR.*

*Then maybe you better wait until I'm off duty.*

*What's going on?*

*Maybe nothing. Somebody cut the lock on the gate up at Giles. The old ferry road. A guy going fishing called it in about an hour after I dropped you off at the put-in. Plus there's some vehicles vandalized up near there, between Giles and the dam.*

*So you're on the lookout. That explains the uniform.*

*They're probably long gone. Likely kids on a joyride.*

*Speaking of kids, I found one.*

*What?*

*Below the Seven Isles—Smith Shoals.*

*What do you mean a kid? How old?*

*He was on a rock in the middle of the shoal. Right there where you have to go through.*

*Was he hurt?*

*Not bad. He's nine, maybe ten. He's not telling.*

*He was alone?*

*All by his lonesome. Wearing a dogged-out life jacket a mile too big for him.*

*That's him?* Tabby looked in the rearview mirror. *You packed him out of there?*

*What else was I supposed to do? I couldn't leave him.*

*You could have waited.*

*I did. More than an hour. You see this weather.*

*You have to take him to the office.*

*Remember a minute ago when I said this wasn't official?*

*I told you I was on duty. There's no way I can not log this, Rea. What do you mean not bad hurt?*

*The river hasn't hurt him, except for some sun. He's got some bruises. He's got two burns, too. The kind we used to have.*

*Well, he ain't us, Rea. He's him. And the chances are pretty danged good he's got a daddy in a panic somewhere close, searching high and low for him.*

*A guy come up the river from the bridge looking for him—a badass in a pretty new johnboat. Pistol in his pocket. Claimed the kid had stolen stuff off a couple of trucks.*

*Catalytic convertors?*

*How'd you know that?*

*That truck I told you about up near Giles is in the same shape. The muffler just hanging.*

*So that's three vehicles in the same mile or two. It's some meth-head. If a meth-head can't steal copper, he goes for cats. He cut that lock, then went down the bank to those trucks.*

*And the johnboat guy just let the kid go with you?*

*I had sent the boy up the bank to pee. He hid.*

*He's run off from home is what he's done. And he's older than ten.*

*Maybe. Two cigarette burns right there.* She poked Tabby's waist with two fingers.

*He's not us, Rea.*

*Tell me how he gets to that rock over the middle of the steps.*

*Maybe it's his grown-up that hit those trucks and the gate at Giles.*

*Johnboat and his posse are looking for a kid, not a grown-up.*

*Posse?*

*There was a boy maybe seventeen or eighteen down at the take-out under the bridge. Wispy goatee. And johnboat said he had buddies up at the shoals coming down the river.*

*Was the kid at the ramp packing, too?*

*Not that I could see.*

*How close were you?*

*I talked to him just like I'm talking to you.*

*And all this time the boy is peeing?*

*I put him out at the bend. Sent him through the woods by the old horse path to the road.*

*You really jumped into this pile with both feet, Rea.*

*I knew you'd get me out of it.*

Tabby snorted. *There goes another promotion.*

Rea said nothing.

*Was the trailer for that johnboat at the bridge?*

Rea shook her head.

*Any vehicle at all there?*

*Not that I saw.*

They sat there for a minute, Rea watching Tabby watch the boy in the mirror.

*So nobody's called in a lost kid?*

*No.*

*Only johnboat is looking.*

*We're keeping an eye out until the Jasper County cops get here.*

*Congratulations. You've found him first.*

*Like hell I have.*

*You know I can't keep him, Tabby.*

*You want him in Family and Children's Services? If I take him, he goes to the county sheriff's and from there to DFCS.*

*Why don't you just take him straight to our old foster mother? Eliminate the middle man?*

*I'm going to pretend you didn't say that.*

*I'm telling you, Tabby. He was in the middle of the shoal. Anybody looking would have to be blind to have missed him.*

*You're assuming too much.*

Rea shrugged.

*There's a lot you don't know here, Rea. His daddy is probably on the phone with the sheriff's office right now.*

*If he was, the deputies would be all over the radio to you rangers the second he hung up. A lot I don't know! I know enough. Those burns and that bruise say plenty.*

*You just make sure you're not reading your own story onto him, Rea. You're out there thinking about your daddy.*

*Odis has got nothing to do with this.*

*They serve you the papers on your daddy's shop?*

*No.*

*I wonder why they can't find the owner.*

*Stay on the danged subject, Tabby.*

*I'm not the one getting off it. Rea—you're not thinking straight. Whoever the boy's mama and daddy are, he's still theirs, whatever they've done up to now. You're all knotted up over the shop, over Odis. It'll be that much harder to hide from those papers playing hero for a kid you don't even know.* Tabby didn't look at her. *Think about it, Rea. Paddling by yourself through the Seven Islands and ducking that deputy about the shop—and now we're talking about a lost boy.*

*Exactly. A lost boy. Not my daddy and not the shop.*

They watched him through Tabby's back window. His attention was bent on the truck seat beside him.

*What's he doing?*

*Looking at my tapes, probably. I had a bag of them under his seat.*

*He don't act like a lost kid.*

*He acts like a found one.* Rea sighed. *Let me leave him with you, Tabby. Just for an hour or so. Until somebody calls for him.*

*You leave him with me, I have to call it in.*

*Tell me what to do, Tabby.*

*I just did.*

*Not foster care. There's got to be something else.*

*Brenda and Rafe was twenty years ago, Rea. She did time. It's a different system now.*

*I can't help it, Tabby. Giving him to DFCS—I'd rather have left him on that rock.*

*You just don't want the deputies serving you with those papers.*

*Yeah. I kidnapped a kid to keep from climbing out of an $80,000 hole.*

*Has it ever occurred to you they might be looking for you for some other reason?*

*They're not.*

*You even know who it is looking for you?*

*I don't care who it is.*

*Your old prom date. Jack. You ought to let him catch up to you.*

*He will soon enough. I don't need to make it easier for him.*

*Jack doesn't have the papers, Rea. It's that new, bean-pole cop that has them, Skinner. He's the one talked to me. Would it really be so horrific if he did serve them? Get it over with. Let it go. Hell, it's already gone.*

*Not until they drag me in that courthouse it's not.*

*You talk to Jack. He's got his own reasons for trailing you.*

*You know something you're not telling me.*

*Talk to Jack.*

*My last talk with Jack had too much tongue in it, thank you.*

*That wasn't your last talk with him and you know it. He knows better now, Rea. He knew enough to talk to me to find you.*

*He's still got those same hands.*

*He got your dad's old safe open, Rea.* Now Tabby was watching Rea carefully. *He paid some ex-con from Mableton. Said the guy put one end of a dowel on the safe door and the other in his ear and had it open in five minutes.*

*And there was a million dollars in it.*

Tabby snorted. *Confederate, maybe. Or wampum.*

*What, then?*

*I don't know. Whatever it is, it's yours as long as you have it before you get served.*

*This is something they cooked up to get you to talk me in.*

*Then how come Jack left a box with your name on it on my front steps last night?*

*Why didn't you say that in the first place?*

*I got my reasons. I wouldn't think they'd be hard to figure out.*

*You thought I had something going with him, didn't you?*

*I don't care why you left this time, Rea. Run from the papers, joyride with Jack. I don't care. You know as well as I do you'll be back. But about this boy, you got to make up your mind.* Tabby looked at her watch, then put her hand on the shifter. *I'm due to go get pictures of that gate they rammed. There's nobody in the DNR office.* She unclipped a key from her big ring and handed it to Rea. *You take the boy there and wait. I'll be there in an hour or two acting real surprised to see the both of you. A lot can happen in two hours.*

*What if Jack gets back to the office before you?*

*Jack is not a problem, Rea.*

*Fine. One more thing—wait here a minute. Don't drive off till I wave.*

## V.

Rea shuffled back to her Toyota, looking through the rolled-down window at the boy. He had the bag of cassettes in his lap and was reading the back of one of the cases.

*You want to listen to that one? No, no nodding. No headshakes. You can talk, so talk.*

*Yeah.* His voice was surprisingly deep. *Yeah, I want to listen to it.*

He handed her the tape. Rea slotted it into the deck, then turned the ignition on. A high guitar pealed out of the speakers.

*Mountain Jam. I should have known you'd pick that one. Twenty minutes long and not one word.*

He stared at the tape case.

*You see that ranger there, waiting? It's time for you to tell me what's going on. You don't want to, want to go back to being deaf or whatever, that's fine: you can go with that ranger, right now. But if you're going to stay with me then I'm due some news.*

The boy only went on looking at the names of the songs like maybe he thought the band would tell his story for him.

*I'm Rea. Like I told you back there on the river.*

*I'm Sam.*

*Sam. OK. Who was that in the boat?*

*I don't know.*

*Did he burn you? Did he grab you by the arm?*

*No, ma'am.*

*He can't get at you while you're with me, buddy. You can say.*

*He didn't.*

*Then why did you hide?*

*I just did.*

*Why?*

*I just did.*

*You scared of him?*

*I ain't scared of nobody.*

*You ain't. Hm. Wish I wasn't.*

*He did do it.*

*What? Burned you?*

The boy nodded.

*Made that place on your arm?*

The boy nodded. *Who are you scared of?* he asked.

*You.*

*Me?*

*Of you feeding me a whole string of lies.*

The boy looked at Rea flatly. *He didn't hurt me, but he would if he could. Somebody took something out of his truck. He thinks it was me.*

*When? Where at?*

*Last night. Up close to the dam, where you put boats in the river.*

*The ramp.*

*Down from the ramp, on the other side.*

*All day long I've been telling you old stories. You want to hear a brand new one? I've got a good one about a kid stealing catalytic convertors out of pickup trucks. He's got a burn on his arm where he brushed up against a muffler that was still hot.*

Rea thought the boy might throw the door open and run for it, but he only sat there looking at his hands, the fingernails crescents of grime.

*Usually I'm the watcher. Like that old man in the room of trees.*

*But this time your daddy's arm was too big.*

The boy was a blood tool.

*So you cut out the cats, then you got caught?*

*I only done one. We didn't get caught. Boyce left us. We got back to where he dropped us off and he was gone. We waited a long time. The sun was going to come up.*

*Y'all stole the canoe.*

*He put that life jacket on me. The big one you wore.*

*Then he left you on that rock?*

*He had to. The boat had this fixed place on it that busted on a tree. It was filling up with water.*

*So he put you out on that rock?*

*Not right off. Later. After the motor quit.*

*I though you said he was paddling.*

*You said that.*

*Yeah. I did, didn't I. And you knew better and didn't tell me.*

Again the boy was looking at her, his mouth in that hard line.

*Look here, Sam.* The name felt strange in her mouth. *Straight's got to go both ways. If I'm going to be plain with you, you got to be plain with me.*

The boy turned and stared at Tabby's truck.

*What?*

*You just going to give me to them.*

*No I'm not.*

*You said you was, unless I talked.*

*Well, I wasn't going to. I just said that to try and figure out where exactly on shit creek you and me are sitting.*

*That's not being straight.*

*No. It's not. So we've both gone and messed up once. We're even, right?*

*Right.*

*Straight goes both ways from here on out, right? Right?*

*Right.*

Rea waved at Tabby. The green truck rolled backward, then headed off. Again Rea expected the boy to bolt and again he didn't.

*So here it is straight, Sam.*

*Buddy.*

*What?*

*That's what you been calling me.*

*You like that better?*

The boy nodded.

*Dandy. So here it is straight, Buddy. I'm not going to make you tell on your daddy or whoever—*

*He's not my daddy. He just says he is. He's a stabfinger, like you told me about.*

## VI.

Sam said he had last seen his father disappearing into the woods downstream of the rock islet where Rea had found him. He claimed to have watched the man cross the current to the river-left bank and drag the canoe up into the trees. Rea didn't believe for a second that a swamping canoe with a motor mounted on it and three catalytics inside it had gotten down the steps. The boy was probably protecting his father.

Thunder rumbled as Rea took the dirt Forest Service road toward the DNR office. They jounced down the road, gradually slowing as it got rougher, the river glinting between the sweetgums that sloped down to the water on their left. Near the three-way, gearing down for the turn, Rea was easing off on the clutch when she felt the boy stiffen on the seat next to her and glimpsed a flash of movement through the windshield.

On instinct, Rea hit the brakes. A shirtless, buzz-cut man stood directly in front of the passenger side headlight, his left arm fully extended, the hand wound in white cloth and locked through the windshield on Rea.

*You breathe on that gas pedal and I'll blow your face off.* His eyes flicked to the boy and back to Rea. *Get out, Sam.*

The boy pulled the door handle.

Rea held the man's eyes. She saw his wide pupils, his drawn jaw. *Is this your daddy?*

The boy paused, nodding his head.

*Shut up, you fucking pervert.*

*Or what? You going to shoot me with that t-shirt?*

*You try me.*

*If you hadn't called this kid by name, you'd be under my truck right now, mister. It ain't too late to put you there.*

*Get out, gotdamn it.* The boy pushed the door halfway open.

*Hey, Sam. Buddy, I mean.* From the corner of her eye Rea saw the boy look at her. *You don't have to. It's just like on the river. Decide for your own self.*

*Shut up.* The man was at the boy's door now, jerking it open. *Come on.*

The boy shrank back on the bench toward Rea. She popped the clutch. The truck lunged forward, the passenger door striking the boy's father with a sound like a kicked garbage can, throwing him backward into the dirt.

Rea hit the brakes and turned to the boy. *You sure?*

The boy looked at her. He made a single motion with his head, a bow. A nod, maybe, then, quick as a snake he was out the door with Rea's PFD in his hand, slipping toward the back end of the truck.

Rea threw her own door open, calling him as she stumbled out. Through the haze of dust the tires had raised, she watched the boy's father slowly roll over onto his stomach in the road. He rose on his hands and knees, head hanging and bobbing as he tried to take in breath. His left hand was still wrapped in the t-shirt, dusty now. Rea reached into the truck bed for the paddle shaft, hefting it in both hands as she rounded the tailgate, ready to step between the man and Sam.

The boy had the derringer leveled on him. Gradually, the man came upright on his knees, sitting back on his heels, bowing again and again from the waist as he tried to inhale. Three fleshy knobs like buds of cauliflower made a rough line along his left side under his ribs. Old stab wounds—or maybe gunshots. His eyes moved from the boy's face to the gun barrel and back again. He did not raise his hands.

*Sam*, he croaked. *Little bastard.*

The boy held the pistol with both hands. He cocked the hammer back with his thumb.

Either the man still wasn't breathing well or Rea couldn't hear him over the river, which had grown louder. Breaking on the shoal behind her, its sound drowned out the idling truck engine and everything else. She felt it on the brink of carrying them away—her, the boy, his meth-head daddy, the truck. She was ready to let it. Then she realized that the clouds had given way. It was rain she was hearing. The cold she felt was rain.

Rea saw in the set of their jaws that neither of them would surrender. The father's eyes narrowed as the boy's widened. They both panted.

*After I came back for you,* the man said. *I dare you, you little—*

The hammer clicked on the empty chamber like a snapping twig, shooting a quick, sharp grief through Rea. What she would remember later was the flicker of disappointment on the man's face—a disappointment that had less to do with his son's pulling the trigger than with the fact that no bullet would come. As quickly as the flicker appeared it was gone. Rea barely had time to recognize herself in it.

*You little shit,* the man said. *You little shitass—*

*You were lucky you ever had this boy,* Rea said, the paddle cocked back like a bat. *You wasted him.*

*What will you give me for him?* The man's eyes shifted to Rea. He hawked and spat at her feet. *Dyke bitch.*

*Buddy, hand me that pistol.*

*It's mine.*

*I'll keep it for you.*

The boy looked at the derringer, his knuckles white around the grip.

*You let me take it on the river. Let me take it now. You won't need it with me.*

Rea lowered the paddle. The boy ruefully handed the derringer over. Rea quickly pulled the two shiny brass bullets from her pocket, loading the pistol and closing it in one motion.

*Get in, Buddy.*

Rea backed to her door, her eyes on the man still on his knees. They left him there cursing in the rain and the dirt.

## VII.

Once they rounded the second bend after the three-way, mud spudding the fender wells, Rea had to slow down until the rain slackened enough for her to see clearly. Through his dripping hair Buddy watched her downshift on a curve. She had him slide over to the middle of the bench seat and take hold of the stick. She told him to listen to the engine to know when to shift. Both hands on the knob, his eyes on her feet, he looked fierce. He didn't miss a gear. Rea was impressed.

*Have you done this before?*

He nodded, gripping the knob, his eyes on her clutch foot. He looked like a refugee from a flood. As they drove, his eyes moved back and forth from her feet to the rearview mirror out Rea's window.

Abruptly, they drove out of the downpour into a light shower. The sun shone, then grayed over, then shone again. This manic road brought them out of the woods and between grassy meadows shaded by pines. Weeds swished like current along the fenders as the tunnel of trees ended. Rea turned up the crush-and-run drive toward the DNR office.

Glancing in the rearview mirror, she saw the empty road behind them and was completely exhausted.

Rea had no excuse for acting like a long-lost auntie, a mother. Any minute another bumper crop of white blood cells, her one sure inheritance, could bloom in her chest, her lymph nodes. Where would the boy be then, assuming she took him in? What had gotten into her? Not pity. Anger—at least it felt like anger, the way whatever it was propelled her, pushing her through to a future she couldn't see and didn't trust but that seemed inevitable.

There was nothing to come through *to*. She knew it as well from her father's death as from the running of this river. After beating a rapid, you hit flat water for a time, then another rapid. It was more about resisting in the present than persisting into a future. She didn't want to push through, only to push back. Until she had gotten cancer it had always been a character flaw.

She remembered Odis when she had waked up from the surgery. Rea had been more startled by his wearing reading glasses than by his presence. He had been awake and waiting, though it was after midnight. He must have had the tumor even then, growing, threading red tributaries into his brain. She wondered if it was the tumor that had brought him back to her. Brain tumors caused uncharacteristic behavior, Rea had read—mild men erupting into profane anger, violence, sexual furies. If glioblastoma could drag the meek and mild into depravity, couldn't it also raise your father out of depravity, if that was his norm? Odis had been sober for a year by that point and had not seen her once. She knew he had quit: Koenig had pulled her over in his un-marked car to tell her. For all she knew, the ancient lolly-gaggers in the shop had thrown him a party.

She could have called him and asked why he was stay-ing away, but she had been too afraid that the answer was Tabby, that Odis was ashamed of Rea's loving and living with another woman. Though Rea had said nothing, Tabby had known. *Of all men on the face of the earth*, she had said, *your daddy ought to see perfectly clearly why a woman would want another woman over a man.* They had laughed. After-ward, Rea thought Tabby had said it exactly as her father would have.

Odis had seemed like himself when he had cared for her after the surgery. How Rea could think that when the man had ignored her for so long, living in a bottle, she couldn't say. The evidence was in the way Odis washed away the purple stain of the antiseptic and dabbed on the salve that was supposed to smooth and soften her mastectomy scars. One look under the bandages and Tabby had run from the room—the only time Rea had known Tabby to run from anything. Odis's only worry had been about embarrassing Rea.

*Nothing there to see*, Rea had said. He laughed, which made Rea's temper flare, but only after she laughed, too. Hearing them from the hospital hallway, Tabby had stomped back in, furious, which made Odis hush, which made Rea laugh harder. Nothing was funny. Rea had been laughing in something's face.

Rea had rued and relished that laughter at the same time. It had hurt Tabby. Rea hated that. Rea's loss was more Tabby's than Rea's own, but right after the operation Rea had not figured that out yet—she wouldn't see it clearly until the day they put the prosthetics in Rea's bra while Tabby was down the hall at the coffee machine. When Tabby came back into the room and saw Rea, there were no tears and no running away. No words, either. The look on Tabby's face said it all. Rea hadn't worn a bra since, or grown her hair long.

Buddy wasn't so different from Tabby. If he stayed with Rea, he had more to lose than Rea did. All this time, throughout her cancer and chemo and then her father's, the future had dwindled in value until it didn't matter at all. Everything had come down to the here and now, so that Rea wasn't so different from the desperation cases that came into the pawn shop. The boy reversed all that. He was more than a here-and-now. He was a future. She couldn't live up to this trust she was building in him.

The empty gravel lot at the DNR office hadn't been rained on at all. As Rea tried the door, the boy stood by the truck looking back down the road the way they had come. Rea showed him which of her keys opened the back door and sent him around to let them in while she kept an eye on the road.

Once they were inside, Buddy drifted into the small museum to the right of the doorway, where a glass case held flint points, potsherds, a stone hammer, the skulls of a coon, a beaver, a gar, snake skins, and a bowl of buckeyes. At the end of the case stood a gaping black bear with his paw extended, as if to shake hands. On the far wall hung two wood ducks frozen mid-flight and a wall-sized map of the river valley along with some sepia photos of the half-finished Lloyd Shoals Dam.

Rea eyed the two-way radios in their charger behind the counter. She took her keys back from the boy and gave him a handful of change.

*There's a drink machine through that door and down the hall. Get us both one.* He went.

Rea rounded the counter, pulled a radio from its charger, and said Tabby's name into it. She didn't answer.

The phone on the counter rang several times, then stopped. The radio squawked once, then said *Miss Rea, please answer the damn phone.*

It was Jack. The phone rang again. This time she picked it up.

*Deputy Jack,* she said.

*Hey, Rea. I heard you on the radio.*

*Why didn't you just talk to me on that?*

*Not everything is fit for the radio. And talking to me on the phone like this, you know I'm not in the car closing in on you.*

He was right about that much.

*What is it, Jack? You thinking of proposing?*

*I just wanted to make sure you got the box I left for you. Some stuff of your daddy's.*

*So I heard.*

*Yeah. I had to pick it up as possible evidence, but it looks like it was a dead end, so I figured I would return it to you. I left it at*

*Tabby's place. She's the one took it to the office. I expect she told you.*

She didn't. *She mentioned you were looking for me.*

*Not really. That box, that was it. Your dad, he was a good fellow.*

At the beginning and at the end he was.

*Even sauced he had his moments. He paid for my tux for prom. Did you know that?*

*No, but that's Odis. King of the bad investment.*

*Come on, now. We had us a good time.* I *did, anyway. Sorry if it was at your expense.*

*It wasn't.* Rea didn't know who she was now any better than she had twenty years ago. She remembered Jack's hands, how they had made her hate her breasts. She wanted to feel that hate again, but it was as gone as they were. *Where are you?*

*Up here near Almo's on a call.*

*Somebody stealing crickets and shiners?*

*Funny. A couple of trucks at a river place up here had parts stolen off them. The owner is mad as hell. He's got his kin and half his crew running up and down the river looking for the culprit.*

*I saw some of them on the river—a fat cat in a johnboat. When did it happen?*

*One of the trucks was drove yesterday evening, so probably last night or this morning. I'd lay money some meth-head is on a spree.*

*Makes more sense to steal the whole danged car.*

*Car thieves, they get caught. These catalytic convertors, they're quick cash at the scrap yard. They just slide under the car and saw it out from between the muffler and the engine. It's a tight space, but meth, it keeps them skinny.*

*Well, go catch them. I better go find this box.*

*You do that. May be some cash in there for a rainy day. Like this one here.*

*Maybe. Thanks, Jackie.*

&

Rea found the box on the desk in Tabby's office, open, curls of tape hanging from the flaps. The boy wasn't there. The back door was cracked open.

*Buddy?* Rea rushed back to the front room. Through the glass doors, she saw that the Toyota was gone.

The boy must have had the sense to let it roll back to the edge of the lot before he started it so she wouldn't hear it turn over. She shook her head, then checked her ring: the truck key was missing. If the boy was a blood tool, she was, too.

Rea found no cash in the box except a heavy, zippered vinyl bag she knew was full of coins. There was a shoebox of wrist and pocket watches, and an unbound stack of pictures: Rea's mother half Rea's own age (probably the very year she ran off with the mill boss), Rea herself as a girl in overalls, vaguely familiar strangers in Panama and pillbox hats, her parents' old ramshackle house in the mill village with her father sitting on the top step and Rea barefoot on the bottom, both of them shirtless. Rea went and got the two-way and carried it outside with her.

The sun blazed on the gravel lot. Down the sloping drive, dust hung in the air where the road banked right—away from the river, from the stabfinger daddy, from where Tabby might have headed him off. Where the truck had been parked, an unopened can of Sundrop sweated on four neatly stacked fifty-dollar bills. Rea sat down on the rocks and hefted the cold soda, watching the can's wet circle evaporate from the bills. Two of them were the old design, phased out in '94. On the top one a note had been scrawled in pencil: *Strait goes both ways I heard you call the law.* She told herself the boy hadn't taken anything more than she had offered. She pried open the can. The cold sizzle made her realize how thirsty she was.

# Second Sight

Running the narrow channel around Forty Acre Island, he hit a hung-up sycamore that bounced the kayak toward an undercut rock. As he leaned to brace, the jutting shoulder of fall-line granite thumped him in the temple. There was no blackout, no ringing bell in his brain—just a dull pain, skull against rock, followed by a faint buzzing like a sweat bee against a nylon tent wall. He righted himself, shaking it off, glad he'd had the spray skirt on.

At first he thought the weather had turned—the sky glowering down to the dull, horizon-wide mica-shine that meant storm. Then he saw that his bright boat (Tequila Sunrise, the sticker had named its red-and-yellow swirl) had gone monochrome. The river, too, was black as burned oil, the foam on the standing waves as dull and lightless as mortar mix. He was as absent of color as his granddad's ancient television. Dashing his face with the inky river didn't help. He closed his eyes, opened them, rubbed them. The world seemed composed of graphite and slag.

What could he do but paddle through? He tried, but in grayscale the river's eddy lines and sub-surfaces disappeared: the current grounded and spun him. The dimness felt malevolent. As he passed under the first of two bridges, the span against the flat chalk sky was a long, black shadow, an underbelly alive with the chittering of bats he could perceive only as a teeming overhead seethe. He knew they must be bank swallows, but couldn't convince himself. He saw what he saw. When two dozen swarmed from their unseen mud nests above him it was all he could do not to panic. Against a glaring patch of sky the veering wings flickered, appearing and disappearing like ghosts.

Just past the second bridge, its abandoned roadbed leaking spats of what passed for light onto the shaded flow in ripples that sickened him, he pulled the spray skirt and saw his legs, gray as a dead man's, the hair stark as black wire. The pallid sand of the shallows made a soft sucking sound against his keel. Again he shut his eyes. He beached, got out. He slung his head side to side, up and down, went to his knees in prayer toward the Mecca of color, forehead to the damp riverbank. Nothing worked. He thought of whacking himself with the paddle.

*Is you hurt?*

The voice came out of the yawning darkness under the end of the bridge. He asked who was there.

*Nobody. Just me fishing.*

*I can't see you.*

*You eyes—they failing on you?*

*I hit my head.*

*You see me now?*

*You're under the bridge. I can't see anything under there.*

A shadow moved against darker shadow, its edges indistinct until a pair of black rubber boots became clear, weaving down the slabs of rip-rap that shelved up to the old roadbed. First he saw the calf-high boots, then sturdy knees and thighs carrying wide, round hips in denim overalls, maybe black, maybe new and blue. A woman, her head and face invisible within a big straw hat. A walking stick in her left hand found the short steps. His warped vision made the pattern carved on it a snake's.

*You seeing me now?* Her right hand held a cane fishing pole as upright as a flagpole or spear.

*I see most of you. Not your face.*

She came on, slow with age or caution, until she could have touched him with the pole.

*This close as I'm coming, mister.*

*That's fine. I see you, ma'am.* But he saw only her black eyes against her white sclera.

*What ail you?*

*I can't see right. There's no color. Everything is black or white.*

*Everthing is? Sure enough? Nawsir. Not everthing.*

He realized there was no white, only the bleached gray of dry bone.

*Everything's shadows. No color.*

*How long?*

*I don't know. Forever, it feels like.*

*Something ain't bit you? Something ain't knocked you in the head?*

*A rock hit me here.* He touched his temple, feeling the bone socket through his fingertips, but not feeling the fingers with his head. *In that rapid inside Forty Acre.*

*You laid down yet?*

*No ma'am.*

*You lay down. Lay down, that same rock you pillow.*

*It was in a rapid. It was part of the island.*

*Then you find you one like it. Rock took it. Rock can 'turn it back.*

*I already thought of whacking my own head again, if that's what you mean.*

*I said what I mean. You lay down.*

So he did. He was on his knees still, a flat, foot-wide rhombus of granite within reach of his head. He stretched out, putting his temple to the stone, freckled and shot with graininess—dark and light specks and every colorless gradation between, from pencil lead to pen ink. Charcoal, soot, ash-tipped reed—every medium hands had ever scribbled in. No hint of color and yet too much to see, to read. He rested his head on the hardness, the thin skin alongside his eye still numb.

The woman's head and face above him were a black halo against the sky. For the first time, he feared something other than this dead world he had crossed into. Her stick from the corner of his eye seemed to twist and slither. He closed his eyes.

In the dream his stone pillow was brought to him on a short wooden paddle. The rock was rounder—almost spherical, the size of a large orange—but it was his pillow. The surface, too, was like an orange's, minutely pebbled, glossy. He lay still looking at it, his eye entering each dimple on its roundness, then seeing past the stone to the paddle, carved with curving lines that extended from a circle hidden by the stone. A translucent leathery wing was spread over his sight.

He blinked. The stone had become an alabaster orange, halved—a wheel, white-spoked. At first, its segments were as rust-black as old, dried blood. Gradually they glistened and grew red, his heart lurching at the color. A lost heat rekindled in his blood. The orange began to turn counterclockwise, slowly, a moon. Then it wasn't moon, orange, or stone that was turning, but him. He moved in a circle around it, warmth bathing his left side as if from a fire, bathing his chest, his cheek, and the temple that had struck the rock.

He woke, a weight holding his eyes shut—the woman's large, warm hand, rough with riverbank, smelling of bluegill, worm, gardenia hand lotion. Her long middle finger spanned his eyelids, her other fingers his brow and upper cheeks. He felt the calloused ridge of her palm draped along his temple, as soft on that side of his head as the rock was hard on the other.

*You keep them eyes shut*, she said.

The hand drew away. He heard riprap shift as she went back up the bank—heard her call from under the bridge, *Look now. Look at Old-Mulgee first.*

He cracked his eyes like a sleeper waking into light. He saw the river—clod-colored, flowing under a still, dim reflection of the clouds—then the gray-mottled sycamore trunks of the far side, then the brown-shot, green-and-yellow spatter of their leaves. Beyond, the sky: blue.

*Thank you*, he said, to the clouds, the trees, the water, the woman, who was gone. He was too glad to cry.

# A Ferry and Four Keeper Holes

The stranger came down the river the day after it started to drop, riding on an eel-skin guitar case that floated so high the water seemed to shun it. Hetchy, smoking on the ferry before he had yet hauled across his first wagon of the morning, saw the case before he made out the slender man being dragged along just behind it. Hetchy, like all ferrymen a plucker of flotsam, especially alert after high water, had gaffed the case's handle before he saw the wet haint trailing.

He let bodies go by unless there was bounty involved—burying was a bother in the stony ground—but having hooked him Hetch, swearing, dragged the stranger in.

The body stood the second Hetch's hook pulled him to the shallows—or rather he grew out of the water. There was no scrabbling to get boots under him. Of a sudden he was standing there, the shoulders of his black frock coat already beginning to dry. Hetch swore later that steam rose from the wool.

The Widger sisters Priscilla and Aquilla, preacher's daughters and backsliders both, would deny it. They stood at the crest of the bank where the road began to slope down to the river, having just finished the first half of their morning constitutional. They had not yet made the turn toward the shingle parsonage (claimed as theirs by inheritance two years prior) when they saw Hetchy poling. Priscilla thought the case was a youth's casket washed down from Jackson and hoped to write a poem. Already she had conceived the dead child inside as a foundling of Charon, water-tendered in his tight raft toward who knew what hereafter. For Aquilla's part, there was no knowing what she thought, ever.

The stranger's beard shone black with river—a mask that covered only his lips and chin and that framed the cool smile he gave Hetchy briefly and the Widgers for longer. He was upright in a regal, Castilian way. Also sword-thin. His beard would not dry all day.

Hetchy said, *Your box.* The stranger rising had not held on to his case and now, turning like a compass needle on the eddy side of the ferry, it nosed downstream.

He said nothing, only shifted his narrow eyes toward Hetchy, then back to the Widgers. The case—more alligator than eel when seen closer—drew taut a fine antique chain that popped from the water with a small spray. It was bound, oddly, at the man's ankle.

This was more than Hetchy wanted to see. No soul right in its mind went on the water chained to anything. Hetch cast off the dock line from the clay-bank stump, rang his bell, and was hauled out into the stream. The ferry line creaked as the mule on the far bank trod his circle, spooling the barge over. Drops flew as the hawser tightened.

Alone with passers-through, the Widgers often toed the edge of propriety. Priscilla relished testing the borders of transgression and seeing the shock. Her way was to linger on the brink of sin as long as resident witnesses were absent.

*We are Prissy and Ack,* she said. *You are welcome.*

*To what?* The stranger's oddly ordinary pitch of voice was a teamster's, talking ox-wagons of heart pine down the road and onto the ferry to be floated, contraband, across to Indian side, but an odd enunciation haunted it.

Priscilla opened her mouth but not before Aquilla said, *To whatever you want.*

The stranger looked at Priscilla as he answered Aquilla.
*You ask Rodrigo Ranjel to ask?*
*I tell him to.*

*My sister is mercurial, Mr. Ranjel,* Priscilla said, trusting the word would prove she was a poetess. *She is just now not herself.*

*Nor will I be later, after dark, in the shingle house next to the church.*

*Ackie!*

*This is all the day away,* the stranger said.
*Lets a man build up.*

*Your invitation I shall accept if you but listen to me play. Will you?*

*Is that what packs your fence post?*

*Rodrigo Ranjel pays back favors, on his honor.*

*It won't be me you owe, but Prissy.*

*That pleases him the same.*

Priscilla, aghast, could only gape, hating the stirring in her skirts.

The stranger unlatched his case where it floated on the face of the leaving water. It opened like a river mussel, the lining crushed crimson velvet. Sunk inside slept a blond, gut-strung Andalusian guitar. Its dark port caught and held the faint seethe of the Indian side's eddy like a plucked chord, though neither Widger quite knew she heard this. The stranger raised it by its slender neck, turned it, and strummed, still standing in the shallows.

One string spoke up and down the scale. Then another, alongside and over the first, and another after. The tune wove and swelled, tributary threads streaming, separating, re-meeting, tumbling down drops, standing in waves. It carried more than could be parsed or caught, toying with unspeakable rot at its bottom, flushed funk of an age, its surface all glissando. Merry roil of the dead. The sound wet all it touched, stirred silts to thickening life. It crested and ebbed, opening and spreading into something tidal and estuarine, rich and eager to suck into its soft delta all that long rain and fall flood brought.

The guitar's final minor chord fingered Priscilla lightly and precisely. Heavy blood moved up her calves, through her shoulder blades. She felt her pulse surge against her stays. Her hinges prickled.

The stranger looked only at Aquilla. Outrage and arousal threatened to sweep Priscilla away. She was untouched, would not be granted touch, and was as ridden and rucked with desire for it as the road inland she stood on. Chastity and hunger bristled in her. Violated and ravenous, fearing her heat because the song had freed it, made it no longer only hers. A sudden will took hold of her. Priscilla dug at the bunched silk of her drawstring purse for the small tin of talcum there.

Aquilla returned the stranger's stare. He stroked the warm strings of the guitar, somehow without sounding them.

*You only talk like—how is it said, a* puta*? You only talk like a strumpet.*

Aquilla did not answer.

*Rodrigo sees he has hushed you.*

Priscilla had wrenched her bag open and reached inside, her breath audible on the moist air.

*You see your own vain twanging.*

Priscilla looked up as the man said, his eyes still on Ackie, *Can she not ask for herself?*

Priscilla raised her dead father's dainty black-powder pistol.

*Prissy is a poet,* Aquilla said.

The stranger stepped from the water up the bank to Priscilla's muzzle until it almost touched his chest.

*Sí. A consummation devoutly to be wished,* he said, his eyes on Priscilla, then on the black octagonal barrel.

His gaze did not feel as Prissy had hoped. An ache and delicious chill arced in her chest exactly where the pistol almost touched his.

*Wished,* he repeated. *You heard the longing in the last chord, yes?*

*Tramp,* Priscilla said.

*Hate what you want only after you have had it.*

*Papa's pistol isn't helping, Prissy.*

As if in answer, the ferry bell rang on the white side of the river. Hetchy would be returning with a fare. Priscilla put the pistol back in her purse.

The question among them was what the hate would do after the wanted thing was had—but the far-bank bell already was bringing out the storekeeper Percy and his wife and others beside.

The Widgers turned and went back the way they had come.

The stranger sat on a rock by the ferry ramp, his blood-red case open before him as he began again to play. Around him all day as he plucked and strummed there clung a damp sense of night. His clothes did not dry. The two dozen souls of the ferry hamlet detected it, as did the riders of the ferry across the current, the liminal song gradually growing in their ears until the chords dawned on them midstream.

There was secrecy in his playing, a hiding place. The wheelwright and blacksmith Veerie dwelled most of the morning on the midnight he had spent on a huge white stone up at the shoal watching two Hitchiti girls sit waist-deep downstream, below a waterfall. When the stranger's hand-heel thumped the box, Veerie heard again their rum-crock slosh. Their hope was that their menses, intensified by the full moon, would curse the ferry settlement that had rooted on their side of the river. Of this hope, Veerie knew nothing. His wish for work to tax his body, tense with desire, was granted at noon in the form of a broken wagon spoke.

The wagon-driving woman brought the spoke to Veerie, then sat on the store porch with her berry-red birthmark of a left cheek turned to the stranger playing down by the water. Skinny, scorch-faced, frizzy-haired, the three strands of beard on her chin made her person seem within the realm of possibility for any male. She took the tuppings she wanted, sometimes trading in them for bacon, hoop cheese, rifle shells, or the smithing of a clevis for a singletree. Hers was a solitary, comfortable sufficiency. For her, the song the stranger's six-string's empty body held and sustained was her pine-slab cabin on Wise Creek, clay floor swept clean.

Hearing the stranger's cascading hammer chords, the two boys in town—one true, one tom—soured on yesterday's trade of a jackknife for marbles, but neither would welsh on a deal by saying so. The cat's eyes lay dead and dull in one's palm. The Barlow, forbidden by a mother sure to find it, burned the pocket of the other. By evening, the true boy's right eye was black. Each was bitter with having what he had already had back.

Unspoken among the churchgoing men was their urgency to sell the stranger whatever he would buy, then push him on his way before dark. His music clouded their motives. The youngest among them, to be ordained a deacon the next Sunday the circuit brought the new preacher through, coveted the stranger's instrument, imagining it would draw to the crossing a fiddle, a banjo, and a caller of dances, though he knew his standing among those who mattered would have depended on his bullying such a band out of town. By the time their traded glances and a mute electricity in their shoulder muscles brought the churchmen together at the steps of the store just before twilight—the hooper, the doeskin factor, Percy, the chordwood cutter, and the flatboat owner—the stranger was gone. The men looking down the road where it vanished into the river saw the rock where the stranger had sat, barer than before.

All at once they heard what was missing—the tarantella of notes—the deacon-to-be missed it especially, and their suspicions gradually grew so sharp that in the dark hour before the next dawn, the trysting hooper and woodcutter, seeing the stranger's shadow against the Widgers' kerosene-lamp-lit window as he left the parsonage they had stolen from the town, would seize and question him, then the hooper would kill him after the stranger offered them Rodrigo Ranjel if they would listen to him play. When the woodcutter's cane knife cut him down, it was later said, he bled only river water.

Aquilla would hear the murder from the back stoop where she had shed her clothes and sat down, her own wetness meeting the dampness of the board steps by which the stranger had just left. Aquilla had not been touched all the waking night—had never been touched in her life, could not be touched, as the stranger's chords had proved to her, dead reckoning to her her distance from Prissy—Prissy, whose bodily gratification was the grave of her soul. A grave Ackie had savored digging, for her sister's shame aroused her.

Aquilla listened in the unquiet—black morning's rub of woodsy gristle, the wilds' bored breath between parted teeth, the seethe of the ferry village's greeds—as she had listened in vain at Priscilla's keyhole for long-craved humiliations, for something more than hoarse female breath.

Now Aquilla heard even the creak of the ropes and the drops of black water that popped from them as the hooper and woodcutter hauled Hetchy's barge hand over hand, ferrying the stranger's body out to midstream. She heard them argue when they each in turn could find no clasp or way to free the dead man from his case.

There came the splash. The men's voices ceased and the ferry hawser once more creaked until the barge gritted into the bank. Gradually, from the water, then the shore, rose the ghost of a sound, growing—gut strings plucked in the fey dawn, the same chords as the day before. Then the slosh of sword-thin legs, striding to shore.

ళ

Unlike Tell's folks, the railroad tracks and the river were always there. The tracks ran between the house and the river, on the other side of the dirt road. The river just ran, turtles climbing out of it onto rocks and stick-ups, bream bedding in the eddies in May, bees sucking water from the wet sand in the hot summer. He learned to lead a swooping bank swallow and drop it with a single BB. Later he learned to bowfish with cane arrows he made himself.

To Tell, the river was *there*, an almost-still place where the Towaliga met the Ocmulgee. The railroad tracks were everywhere else. The steel got harder and looked faster with every engine that rolled down it, the tonnage thrumming and creaking behind them boxcar by boxcar. Tell would hear the whistle and go stand at the yard's edge, feeling the air prickle with the power of the freight. He stayed rooted there from the passing of the engineer framed in his window until the caboose chuckled by with its lone passenger leaning out the high window or on the back deck. To turn away before the whole train passed felt like bad luck. The year the railroads retired all the cabooses, each train seemed amputated—a snake with no tail, a book with the back cover torn off. Trains didn't end but quit. Seven times in fifteen years Tell saw riders between the engineer and the caboose crewman—gaunt men, always in caps and coats sitting in the boxcars. Once, Tell saw a boy atop a flatcar of pine trunks. After a train passed Tell would watch the river until he could hear it again.

Tell joined the navy because he was a boy of creek banks and pond docks. The ocean was no pond, he knew, but more home to him than the rice paddies and jungles the army would have dropped him into. But the navy, it turned out, took Tell away from the water.

They trained him to listen. Hyper-tight headphones pinging and crackling, his ears ferreting out voices, ghosts of code, radar signatures. Trying to catch all he could wrung him like his mother's dishrag. For a six-hour shift he sat with five other sailors, all tuned to the same signal. Each day they'd lop off the weakest listener. Next shift there would be one new guy. The listeners were forbidden to talk to each other. By the third day (it might have been night: they were underground) an exquisite pain bloomed in Tell's right side.

It was as if he put it on with the headphones. He ignored it—went on listening as he had before, thinking of the train back home diminishing in the distance and waiting for the slop and seethe of the river to come back to him.

Tell went to the range to relax. He would breathe himself still, his cheek to the stock. Wait. Then squeeze. There was no listening, only punching himself through the tunnel of the scope into the target, as he had shot snakes on the Towaliga and floating milk jugs that circled erratically on the gyre of current where the creek met the Ocmulgee.

At the range, ammo was free. He fired whatever they would give him.

His fifth visit, the range master gave him a rifle with a baffle around the barrel and a can of long, small-caliber cartridges. Tell ticked through them, the gun nearly silent. No kick.

Three days later when Tell reported for his listening shift, the range master stood in front of the bunker door, with him a Marine Corps colonel in crisp fatigues. The colonel unrolled thee targets and pointed to four figure-eight holes which lined up on each silhouette, about where the eyes would be.

*These your rounds, sailor?* the colonel asked.

*Yes sir.*

The colonel tipped his head toward the range master.

*Deadeye here says all your shots overlap.*

*Not all, sir.*

*All with the De Lisle*, the range master said. He walked down the hall to the stairwell door. As it closed behind him, the colonel looked Tell in the eye.

*I know all there is to know about you, sailor. Now I'm assigning you to duty for your country no one can ever know about. Not mama or daddy, not your high school sweetie. They'll write you on a carrier you'll never see. Your assignment will be radio counter-intelligence but you'll never put on those damned ear-muffs again.*

If anything happened to him, they'd say he fell off the carrier.

Tell became a specialist: targets on water. In longboats and deck chairs. On bicycles rolling over bridges. One on a float in a swimming pool. All kills except four who failed to show up where they were supposed to. Not one saw Tell. Not one did Tell hear. He waited hours—days, sometimes, often with the De Lisle set up so Tell's motions at trigger time would be minimal. As he waited, Tell would call back every detail of the river and creek he could—turning catalpa worms inside-out and fishing them on the bottom, finding a silver ring in the gut of a shoal bass, hanging in the air for that breathless quarter of a second after he let go of the rope and before he dropped toward the water. Once the target arrived, Tell would settle himself by picturing the trains passing in slow motion and focusing on the lettering on the cars and on the turning of their wheels. The boy Tell saw on the flatcar that one time had trotted on all fours down the top pine trunk so that for a few seconds, by running the log, he had stayed even with where Tell stood. Then the end of the car had stopped him and he was carried off, staring at Tell until the distance swallowed him. Once Tell scoped the target in, he became this boy.

Now Tell lives there alone, at the crux of creek and river, in the old house. He no longer hears the trains, not even those nights when every other sound wakes him. Disability has bought him a silver canoe and the far bank of the creek so he can keep to himself. He often sits in his boat as it turns and turns where the two currents meet, constantly leaving and constantly holding him in place. Tell feels the boy's eye, feels his aim, and grows calm.

This is Tell's story that no one knows.

᪐

Starr sold her husband's clothes at a yard sale the week after he died. There was late frost on the ground and she didn't place an ad or put up signs on the street corner. If Starr had put up signs they'd have had one word on them: widow. He had fallen while fishing.

Starr sat on the top step of the porch in her robe. Ray's suits hung there in the dogwood, drab next to the white blossoms, under them a low, short wall of folded jeans and sweatshirts on the white grass. Starr had pulled a sheet of plastic from a closet for a ground cloth, but had put it back. It was spattered with the four different paint colors they had tried to brighten the living room with their first week in the house. She didn't want it in the dirt.

The rail-thin man who bought the suits was on foot and didn't come until ten, but he was her first customer.

*They don't have prices*, he said. *How much for the whole tree?*

Two of the four suits had been with Ray longer than Starr had. There were also a fur-lined topcoat too warm to actually wear in Macon, a corduroy sport coat, a glen plaid blazer, and a hanger of neckties. There was a tuxedo Ray had worn only once.

*You need the whole tree?* Starr asked.

*I don't know about* need, he said. He looked like he did know about it—like he personified it in his colorless, rolled-up pants. Instead of a jacket he wore multiple shirts, the outer one denim, with snaps. Ray would have felt for the guy. Ray felt for everybody. Starr had hated that and now she hated that she had hated it. She hated Ray for leaving her in the front yard with a tree full of forty shorts and frost. Who gets killed by a bass?

*They're good suits*, she said. *That blue one got him two jobs.*

The man gripped the shoulder of the navy suit. With his other hand he rubbed the worsted cuff of a sleeve between his thumb and fingers. His back to Starr, he looked like he was shaking hands with the invisible man. He raised the suit from the branch by its hanger, hefting it, then let it back down.

*How much do you want?*

Starr wouldn't be able to sell it. She thought of the breast pocket inside it, holster for Ray's wire-bound memo-book and the disposable click-pencil that he liked to refill.

*Take it*, she answered.

*I'm not a charity case.*

*What kind of case are you?*

He only looked at her.

*You're a suit case*, Starr said. She laughed without making a sound.

He came over to her, suddenly thrusting a hand deep into the pocket of his too-big pants. The motion would have alarmed her if she had been her old married self, but her sense of danger was shot. At the foot of the steps the man drew from his left pocket a wad of bills—a wad of individually wadded bills.

*It needs to cost something*, he said. *It's a gift.*

*I'm not wrapping it.*

*I don't need it wrapped.*

*I don't think it's right as a gift*, she said.

He started sorting the bills, straightening each of them. *How much for the whole tree?*

*Are they all gifts?*

He smiled, showing smoker teeth. *Ever' one*, he said.

*Take them*, she said. *Fifteen for the whole lot.*

*Fifty.*

*Forty. Not a dollar more.*

*Can I try them on?*

*They're gifts for* you?

*For my mother. For her to see me in. At church. I'm going to have to go for two months at least.*

*The door's open.*

He would go inside. He would change in the guest room where Ray had dressed each day, where these clothes had hung in the closet. She could see him there, his need, could see him putting one leg and then the other into the pants, pulling them up.

*Is it anybody else in there?*

*My husband is sleeping.*

*Where?*

*Just go in the first door on the left. You'll be fine.*

He stepped around her where she sat, keeping a respectful distance. She looked at the other clothes on the tree, at the burnt notch in each wide-open dogwood petal.

Starr couldn't decide whether the word *widow* was open or closed, whether there was a difference.

When she turned, he was standing with his back to the front door, the suit over his arm. He hadn't gone in. She felt glad and sorry at the same time.

*You can't pay me for them unless I know they fit.*

*You don't want me in your house, lady. I don't belong in nobody's house.*

*How bad can you be? You're buying them for church.*

*I'm who church was made for. Jesus H. Christ's worst-case scenario.*

*You want your mother to be happy. Think how she'll feel if the pants are too short.*

He might steal everything. She could never be that lucky.

*Try it or don't buy it*, she said.

In the end, he tried the suit on just inside the front door. Starr watched the brief, vague flash of his pale legs through a corner of the living room window.

When he opened the door and stepped out, she was startled. The suit fit him perfectly. He filled it. His innermost shirt was white and clean, if missing the second-to-top button. The sight was like a blow to the center of her chest. Nothing broke but something began to seep.

*You're changed*, she said.

He held out the bills. Starr took them numbly.

*You should wear it home.* She took the clothes he had arrived in and bagged them with the other suits and coats.

*I thank you.*

*My best to your mom.*

Starr watched him diminish down her side of the street until he was a small, familiar shape, a size and shade of blue she knew, crossing the road. For the first time she felt the cold.

క్

The fog swallowed him up so suddenly on his long run he'd have panicked if his abrupt halt hadn't let a bead of sweat burn a crystal-clear hole in the cloud that otherwise surrounded him. He'd left his reading glasses on. Swearing at himself but secretly pleased he could steam up spectacles on so cold a morning, he stowed them in his jacket pocket and ran on.

Two hills later they bounced free in front of the senior citizens' center where sixteen people who still had their glasses on didn't spot them in the grass along the sidewalk. A nun walking to tea scooped them up. Intuiting their neededness, she hooked their earpieces on either side of a slender cherry trunk, where she thought they would be easier for their loser's weak eyes to see.

Several people laughed passing the cherry. A man in his late sixties, a widower for a year and a day, thought what all a tree rooted in place might see in a day—his first solitary silliness. A cheerleader with a fast, rare form of glaucoma glimpsed them from inside her mother's minivan and saw in them God's sympathy.

The specs weren't a sign of grace but an outright gift to the bridge-dweller who plucked them off and put them on. He spent the afternoon reading his bedding. So august did he look behind the little moony lenses that the cop at the door let him into the public library that evening. He washed and relieved himself, taking a pocket full of toilet paper. He read Ayn Rand. At closing time, outside the door, the voices said, *You shat. Good. Now take a bath.* When he laid face-first in the Ocmulgee upstream of his home bridge, in a shallows that looked muddy from above but that was actually clear, the glasses fell to the sandy bottom.

For days the runner reran the route, swerving toward every glint in the morning sun, wanting his vision back. They had fit so well, their framelessness making them almost invisible to others. Searching for them, he saw every shine in the storm gutter and among the weeds. He saw the ground.

The river bottom wore away constantly, though it stayed granular and amber, like the gingery sugar the nun stirred into her tea. The specs rested, polished steadily by a clear blur of current. They still wait to be found.

*ও*

Once his fingers reach the dewy grass to unplug the ancient electric mower—a $20 yard sale find four years ago—Clay will be mown down himself. The coffee (what pleasure) he has just sloshed onto his hand will meet the wetness on the extension cord's plug and the nimbus of ground fog around him: across the slight gap where male meets female a minimal lightning amplified by the water in the air will arc. The cloud of wetness will kill him. He will die because he is barefoot (what pleasure) on the wet earth, because he has procrastinated about putting the mower away, and because he and Eve bought this fixer-upper on the banks of Echeconnee Creek and updated all the outlets except the ungrounded ones outside.

The vim of his toes and his high arch meeting the trimmed wet fescue has called back to him his childhood along with a line from Walt Whitman spoken aloud from memory by his favorite college professor, not in a classroom but in a canoe a few miles above where the Amicalola met the muddy Etowah. The clearer river had just half-drowned Clay in a foaming shoal as Dr. Loren watched. The rapid had flipped Clay's canoe and drawn him, still inside the capsized boat, into a hydraulic, a keeper hole that churned him under four times before he recalled Dr. Loren's lecture about circular currents and swam for the bottom, where the river's grip on him was weakest. Clay had surfaced beside Loren's boat, in an eddy where the flow slowed and shallowed enough to let Clay stand up. *I am mad to be in contact with it,* his teacher had said, with a cryptic smile. *Old Walt.* The rapid's name was Edge of the World.

The temporary order of his lawn tickles Clay's instep like a girl's tongue. The sensation dispels the bad dream that rocked his sleep: in the dream, his friend Weiss, who had a recurrence of cancer nine years ago and had not returned Clay's phone calls since, stood framed in the attic window of his gaily painted Victorian, grimacing in pain. In the dream, Clay saw Weiss from the street, fought his way through the overgrown, head-high yard to the doorless door, and found the house gutted, rotted in sill and stud, the ruined stairs starting five feet over Clay's head. The place creaked and sang with imminent collapse. Clay shouted for him, but Weiss wouldn't answer.

Clay's mind tingles between short- and long-term memory as the image of his son on a green ball field under the lights the night before swirls up. The boy (ten) is plucking from the air above the outfield's inner edge a line drive that he then fires over the shortstop's head to double-off the runner at second: a play so quick it defied belief. Now the moist turf, as fundamental and alive against Clay's heel as it was against the boy's cleat last night, seems to confirm the grace. The rest of the father's life abides in this pure motion.

Clay feels a charge in the wet air—feels this memory forking a dendrite in his head as his ear catches again the birdsong that just woke him (*Tellhim-no-no-no, Tellhim-go, Tellhim-go*) and his nose smells again the fragrance that was two parts his sleeping wife's herbal conditioner and one part her light dawn sweat under their sheets—an incense that aroused him. (*Morning wood*, Eve had often whispered to wake him during that randy middle trimester.) Today, the morning after the boy's game went to extras, Clay has considerately resisted himself. He has gotten up to stow the mower instead, letting Eve rest.

Clay hears the bird re-sing. His white left foot pins the orange cord to the ground as his right index, middle, and ring fingers reach for the synapse where plug meets plug. He looks up, trying to see the singer in the dogwood, which he thinks of as his reward for letting his girl Eve, who birthed the boy still catching the ball, sleep.

The voltage spun in the dam on the river his creek feeds, the fizzing power that has flowed from power pole to power pole to fill the walls of his home, gathers, coiled.

He will be himself a lightning strike in less than a second—will be grabbed and thrashed by current leaping through him back to the ground—except that he follows that one bird's sound. Is conducted by it, by his ear then his eye, to the misted-over dogwood crest on the bank of the creek, to the fogged-over red flutter that makes his fingers miss the meeting place of the plugs. Clay grasps the cord, pulling it as he rises upright, trying to better see the feathers that are a red beyond red. A wing-flash and the bird (scarlet? carmine?) is gone.

Before Eve wakes up, he must have the right word for the color of the bird. He will pinch an iota of thin air and say, *I came this close to missing it.*

## Skin Trade

One of her three steady clients, the art teacher, had offered Merlinda a job modeling, saying her strong curves and the roundness of her hips were perfect. They held the essence of the old masters, the ruddy glow of Helga. He had even brought a postcard of this Helga woman. She would have needed makeup in Merlinda's profession, and Merlinda said so. But the art teacher kept calling and he kept offering her more to model, though the dates cost the same. One afternoon as he laid across the bed in the carriage house she had been renting and staging as her live-in space for business purposes—his body pale, not a muscle visible anywhere on him, though his smile compensated for it, as he well knew—he started describing her, moving his eyes along her body and sketching his favorite parts in a few words.

*Brown as the best bread. Wine brown as roses. Wine-dark, like in Homer. The tassel on ripe corn. Baked apple—cinnamon, soft. Dusky.*

He had gotten ideas saying that, so it was time to get back to business, or really just let him get back to it, once she gave him the shy, eyes-down face men generally wanted in return for that sort of thing. Afterwards he had asked her again to model. He offered her two hundred dollars for a two-hour session, plus the hundred the art school paid to "life models," which sounded suspiciously like a reference to her age.

*For just you? Nobody else there?*

*Just me. Private studio.*

*No way, then. It's weird. I don't do weird.* It wasn't. Merlinda was seeing what the market would bear.

He kept a cool demeanor, but she sensed he was surprised and confused at being rejected just when he thought the baked apple bit had made her melt. He rallied quickly.

*You mean you* want *other people there? A class?*

*At least then I'd be teaching somebody something. Like trying another vocation,* Merlinda said. She liked the word vocation. It reminded her of high school, when she had taken a class called Careers, walking to a different place to work one afternoon each week. She had made onion rings at a drive-in (the ingredients—milkshake mix and cornmeal—had surprised her), stocked greeting cards at a drug store, watered plants at the feed and seed. She had even learned to check oil and change it. One of her disappointments on coming back to town had been the discovery that all these businesses were gone.

The art teacher smiled and promised he would call.

After he left, Merlinda found an additional fifty under the stoneware cannister in the bathroom where clients placed their fees—either a tip or an advance.

They set it up over the telephone. The next Thursday Merlinda put on new jeans and a white blouse buttoned to the top, parked the Firebird downtown, and rode the bus to the university. She got off at the art school, a big place with a porch held up by brown granite columns. Students in little knots were scattered across the steps. In the middle of the lawn stood a scatter of old bricks and girders and slabs of crumbling concrete—someone making a mess out of some kind of repair, she guessed.

Merlinda spotted the art teacher. He had been waiting just inside the porch and strolled down toward her, smiling, his little rawhide earring swinging.

*Welcome to academia, Vanessa*, he said, using the working name she had picked up from a rich, conniving brunette on "The Guiding Light." He nodded at the pile on the lawn. *Do you like it? One of my students did it—part of his senior project.*

Merlinda glanced back at the jumble of broken brick and twisted, rusty metal.

*It's ok. Is your student German?* Last year, the East German collapse had been the talk of Chicago. She had watched the sledge-hammering of the Berlin wall on CNN in The Auberge, one of the hotel bars she had used for initial meetings with prospective clients. For a month, con men on the Mile had spoken to her from behind propped-open trunks and American Touristers, offering chunks of the wall, always with the same pitch—a piece of history. Some of them had taped photocopied newspaper pictures to their suitcases of rubble as proof of authenticity.

Inside, the art teacher took her to a huge, second-floor room, the back wall one big window, then he went to his office for his things, leaving her standing surrounded by odd benches that had desktops at one end.

Merlinda felt a small, pleasant shock at the early autumn light blazing in. The concrete floor was slick as a movie theater's. In the middle of it was a foot-high, unpainted plywood dais, the nails at the corners still silver.

She felt the first urge of worry. Always know exactly what you're doing, Dena had taught her. Always be two steps ahead. Here, Merlinda was at sea. Years ago, when she had first worked in the city, before she had met Dena and learned how to build and manage a book of decent clients, she had endured some pretty crummy gigs—not the worst, none of what the other girls called dog tricks—but she had acted it out with women, had mimed doing herself, and had worn humiliating outfits. She had been a cluster of grapes, Joan of Arc, Peter Pan, Laura Ingalls, one of those green women from *Star Trek*—everyone but herself. And that had been the secret, just as Dena had said. *On the job, be anybody but you.* It was still the secret now, fifteen years after the best-paying clients in her book, men whose pictures she saw in the *Tribune*, had gone the way of her twenties and her limberness. She just had to be not her*self,* but the body the class required, if she could figure out how to fill that blank.

It worked in more than just the escort business. When Merlinda had come back to Macon to sell her great-aunt's mill house—the lawyer's letter had been the first word from Georgia in twenty years—she had sat in her car and watched the agents coming and going at the real estate office for two consecutive Mondays (the one day desk people really worked all day, all the way, according to Dena). The third Monday, Merlinda had walked in herself, wearing the same-height heels and the same Chaus suit as the first female agent to get there both mornings, and she had gotten the ball rolling on the house sale. The ball was still rolling almost two months later—new roof, new AC condenser, other repairs that had extended her stay to maximize the return on Aunt Neeta's small, sturdy shotgun house.

Merlinda had meant to sell quickly and get back, but hanging around hadn't been as awful as she had expected. Neeta's place had surprised her with good memories: her older cousin Odis teaching her to string cane fishing poles they cut together at the wild edge of the backyard where it backed up to the levee, Aunt Neeta baking cobblers from blackberries Merlinda had picked, being paddled on Odis's tarpapered plywood boat across the river to the sandy beach on the opposite bank to swim. Merlinda had found the levee trail, faint but still there, and followed it up to look from the high bank across the river to the beach with its frowsy border of willows separating it from the woods. She had discovered she could stand there and look at the green of the willow fronds just beginning to fade and the hardwoods behind them showing every shade of yellow and rust and not think at all of her pothead mother's house or the stepbrother who had been Merlinda's reason for leaving. So after a call to an old Chicago friend of Dena's who ran two escort services in Atlanta, Merlinda figured she knew enough about how it worked down south to venture into the marketplace. So far, so good. Competition was so scarce that she had twice been sent flowers by clients. The town was still full of churches, which her Atlanta colleague assured her was good for business. Men of means knew how to read the personal ads and how to buy you an exploratory drink in the bar at the Hilton. Merlinda's marketing to academic types—the males, at least—worked in Macon as it had at U of Chicago and Northwestern, though the client base was much smaller.

The art teacher came back with a paint-splotched wooden tackle box. He smiled broadly at her again. *Want a Coke? Coffee? Anything?*

*No thanks. Where are they?*

*The students? Oh, they'll be here*, he said, busy unloading the box onto a little table beside an easel. *Class doesn't start for another five minutes. You can change in that room to your left there.*

*Why not out here?*

The smile again. *Well, wherever, as long as you're robed before they come in. They're young. It's important to be professional with them.* His eyes met hers in a way Merlinda thought was supposed to look businesslike. Whether in her business or his was hard to tell.

*So I have a few minutes?* she asked.

*Sure. You'll hear the students coming in and settling. Then just walk out and step up there.*

*But what do I do?*

*Do?*

*On the stage.*

He gave her a level look. He had never looked at all like a teacher to Merlinda until now.

*Don't do anything. Just stand there. Here—like this.* He stepped onto the dais, kicked out one black boot a little and held his straight right arm at the elbow, looking down. He relaxed. *Or you can sit if you want. I'll get you a bench or something. I mean, these are first-years mostly, some of them might have trouble drawing you that way, but if you want to sit…*

*No, I can do it standing up. No spreading or anything?*

The smile again, with a glint this time. *Maybe later. But for the class, nothing sexy. Just stand there. Don't look at them.*

The real issue was simple. Merlinda hadn't been personally naked in years—not stark, buck bare, the way she had been at fourteen looking out the window across the alley and through another windowpane into Frank Funderburk's eyes as she was on her way to the bath. She had paused, fully facing the window, watching his gaze, which never moved up to her face. Stupidly, she had walked slowly to the bathroom, pushing her toes, then her heels into the floor as she went. Feel your feet into the floor, she had once heard a ballet teacher on public TV say. She had done exactly that, enjoying the taunt. She still did that whenever a man looked at her, though now she knew where the handle on the power was and how to keep her grip on it. But she already sensed a classroom was different.

જ

*Why shouldn't I look at them? They're looking at me.*

*Well, they're kids, most of them. Like I said, they get uncomfortable.*

*They do or you do?*

*Come on, Vanessa. Time's wasting.*

The dressing room was a closet that smelled of turpentine, lit by one hanging bulb. On the back of the door somebody had painted a single, gigantic, deep blue eye, the pupil as big as a beach ball and the iris so huge that the blue lapped past the door onto the walls on either side of it. The pupil had a long curving white window painted on it to make it look 3D. Maybe she ought to climb out it and head for the Greyhound station, as she had her mother's casement the week before graduation. She had wanted to make it to commencement but had woken up to the stepbrother trying to pick the lock on her bedroom door again, this time with her mother in the house. Like father like son. She looked at the knob on the closet door, remembering the fear she had felt hearing the stepbrother trying to keep the bobby pin quiet in the lock. It dawned on her that, compared to then, she wasn't afraid at all. Nervous, sure, but not afraid.

Merlinda slipped her blouse off and felt the air on her upper arms and shoulders. It always seemed chilly to her until she got everything off, then she reached room temperature and held there and it was all right. Someone had left a white cotton robe hanging on a nail in the wall.

Merlinda heard the students enter—shuffling feet, the mumble of the teacher talking, the dragging of benches, paper warping. She looked the eye in the eye and stepped out of her panties. She let it get completely quiet.

When she opened the door, a dozen students sat on benches around the small stage, all of them turning to look at her as she tried not to walk too fast down the short aisle. The concrete floor jarred her feet. She was used to heels.

Merlinda stepped up onto the plywood, warm and rough against her soles, exactly like Odis's homemade skiff except dry. She came to a full stop—a little stiffly, she thought—with her back to the students, pulling the sash and letting the robe drop. The cool air circulated around her hips and thighs and seemed oddly active. Remembering to breathe, she turned, rounding her shoulders and standing exactly as the art teacher had, looking down at the concrete beyond the edge of the dais. She hadn't thought it was possible, but she was personally naked again.

With a general rustle of paper and scraping bench feet, the students in their sneakers and boots and jeans began to move around her. A boy wearing a ball cap backward stopped to her left, just within her peripheral vision. A girl in some kind of red top and black hose—Merlinda thought they were black, but couldn't be sure without looking— stood right in front of her, sketching in rapid strokes. Merlinda could smell her perfume—Poison. She wore it herself sometimes, but never that much. The other students eddied around her, looking so hard she could feel it, not where she had expected to.

Gradually, they settled, some of them (some of the boys even, that she had expected to move in close, like the men during her table-dancing days) sitting or standing behind her, their pencils and charcoal scratching intermittently at first, then steadily. To relax, Merlinda pushed her mind away, willfully losing her focus on the gleaming floor. The leads against the paper reminded her of grade school—fat red pencils following traceable dotted lines to print letters. As a girl, she had wanted to be a teacher, had lined up dolls and secondhand stuffed animals into rows and taught them. As she thought about it, she half-heard the art teacher among his sketchers, praising a line or stroke here, suggesting changes there. *More shading—shadow makes light.* Once, he said, *Go spelunking.* The only time she remembered her father playing with her before he died, they had played school. She remembered him seated on the floor, a bearded giant next to Care Bear and Holly Hobbie—remembered his hand raised, but not the answer he gave when she called on him, only that it was wrong. She couldn't recall his voice, only, dimly, his holding her on his lap, silently reading Peanuts from the comics page. So many men's laps since and still she remembered that one.

⚬

*Okay, that's one*, the teacher said suddenly. Merlinda looked up from the floor and he met her eyes. *Thanks. Ready for a break?*

She walked around the dais, looking down at the plywood. The art teacher brought her a cup of coffee, waved her down toward a stool.

*See? That wasn't so bad, was it?* He set a stool on the dais and waved her to it.

*I guess not. I thought it would last longer.* The stool was cold on her ass. She hesitated, thought about sitting on her hands, then saw that the art teacher was holding the robe out to her.

*It depends on what's being taught. This class, they're learning broad strokes, how to see quickly and get it down before their brains interfere.*

*Oh. So can I see what you've done so far?* She looked at him straight, naked. It was a look she had created to make her nakedness into a kind of brassy armor: payment due when service rendered.

*I would love to show it to you, but it's all up here.* He tapped his temple. *I mean, maybe you noticed—I've been teaching?*

*I heard you, yeah. Calling them by name.* She could tell his focus had split between her and the dozen-odd college kids. *I just wondered. You were so up for this.*

*Yes, I was.* He looked at her then away. *It's going great.* But Merlinda knew the look of a man who wanted something he couldn't ask for.

*You're a good teacher.*

*Not really. I didn't think twice about sharing like this.*

Sharing? That was rich.

*It's a little weird—you and them. I don't know.*

*Yeah—work meets play.*

*Usually in art, work is play, Vanessa.*

For a second, she didn't know who he was talking to.

*Don't worry, teach. You don't have to share me much longer.*

*I meant sharing them with you.*

He clapped twice. *That's five,* he said. *Better get back to it, everybody.*

∾

For the next session the art teacher left the stool on the dais and asked Merlinda to step her right foot on a rung and rest her elbow on a knee, chin in palm. She did, choosing a bright yellow ginkgo tree beyond the window to focus on. The students shifted and flipped to new sheets of their pads.

*You have five minutes*, the teacher said. *Find her.*

From the corner of her eye she thought she saw several students smile. She risked a look at a boy straddling a bench near the glass wall. His arm moved in long strokes down the paper. His eyes seemed fixed on her throat. She realized he must be working on her chin and hand. But why the long strokes, then? He looked at her face, almost before she shot her eyes back to her tree.

Five minutes felt like forty-five.

*Okay, last strokes everyone*, the teacher said, strolling between the crooked aisles one last lap. *Now—show her.*

Merlinda looked at him, surprised, but he was walking to the back of the room. A few students looked at each other meekly, then briefly at her. No one came forward.

The teacher turned. *Don't be shy now, people. Whatever you have she gave you.*

There was a small pause of shifting eyes.

*We'll let Vanessa come around and see for herself. Touch up if you like. After we've looked at your piece you can go.* He offered Merlinda a hand down from the dais as if it were some kind of carriage. She looked at him, cocking an eyebrow. She let the laughter ripple around the room, mostly among the girls, then accepted the hand and stepped down, her feet slapping a little on the floor. She shrugged into the robe the art teacher offered and loosely tied it.

No two of the drawings were of the same person and none of the first several she saw even seemed to be of her at all. The Poison girl's was a series of three, all on the same page, all with a crossing of two curves where there should have been a nose and a mouth, though the hair was Merlinda's. Another girl's had only a few sinuous lines for the body. Everything below the detailed, lifelike, unfamiliar face was as vague as if underwater. The backward-cap boy had sketched her mascara and lipstick in dark, thick lines, erasing in key places to show the lips' shine, shadowing her jawline and ear while leaving her body a whiteness except for the dimple of her navel and an ebony vertical strip for the Brazilian wax. Another boy, wearing his long hair in a bun, his pencil dented all over with toothmarks, had done something striking in shading Merlinda's (yes, they were hers) cheeks and upper lip; she suddenly realized they were flushed—she had sweated. A second version of her from the opening session was simply her shoulder and left arm down to the hand, the elbow clasped in her right fist. It was her fist, her knob of an arm joint visible in the way the fingers held it. Merlinda nodded and smiled as she walked from bench to bench. The many alternates of her drowned out the art teacher's pointers. She was glad when it was over.

The art teacher had said he would give her a ride back to the carriage house, but Merlinda caught the bus instead. Better to make him wait a bit. Better to clearly separate posing from other paid services. She had boarded, sat down, and begun to sort through all the odd other selves she had just seen—like mutant twin sisters that hadn't survived—when she looked up and found herself almost toe to toe with the lanky boy in the ball cap, his tackle box in hand, a book-bag on one shoulder. He was smiling.

*Thanks for what you said about my sketch. Do you mind if I sit down?*

Merlinda slid over. Dena would not have approved.

*You were so fun to draw. A great change of scenery from the guy we had last week. He was really skinny. Once you got his angles down, he was a snooze.*

*Thank you, I guess.* Merlinda wasn't sure what to make of him.

*I didn't mean that in a bad way. I just prefer curves and contrast, you know? You're the first I've sketched with makeup on.*

*Posers don't wear makeup?* She immediately regretted the question.

*I don't know. Most I've seen don't. But I love the way it adds a challenge—drawing what somebody has painted, you know? See what's underneath, then layer the color and high-lights. That's tough with just charcoal.*

Merlinda looked out the window doubtfully. Looking silly was dangerous in her profession—fatal on the street, where she hadn't been since those three weeks before she turned eighteen. Two seconds without keeping your sharp edge out could end you, Dena had said, often. Once, when

Merlinda had rolled her eyes, Dena had removed her perfect front teeth. You think I worked while this was healing?

*Did I say something wrong? Really, the makeup was no big deal. One time a girl I'd been trying to talk to for weeks drew me with a zit like an iceberg on my chin.*

Merlinda looked at him. *You've posed?*

*A few times. When I needed the money.*

*But only when you needed the money?*

*I'm not crazy about being naked in front of a crowd.*

*A jury of your peers.*

*That's a good one. Seriously—I admire people who can do it so calmly.*

*Did you ask her out?*

*Who?*

*The girl who drew your zit.*

He looked away. Half smiled.

*I mean, the woman didn't just put in my acne. She* added *to it.*

*But you don't have acne.* Merlinda felt herself click firmly back into control. *She saw you butt-naked and you freaked.*

He actually laughed, which surprised her. She had been about to say *No shame.* He didn't feel any anyway.

*Next stop is mine.* He stood. *I hope you do another session.*

*I pose for private sessions, too.*

*That's cool, but way out of my budget.*

*What's your budget?*

*Like, negative zero. College kid, you know.*

*Oh, of course.* She didn't know. They could afford school, couldn't they? Poison wasn't cheap.

*I'm Bryan.* The bus brakes hissed and the doors flapped open. *Hi and bye.* A wave and he was out just before she almost said her real name. Dena would not have been happy.

๑

A week later, against her better judgment, Merlinda was back at the art school, doing the second of three sessions of modeling for an oil painting class. The phone messages from her Chicago clients had fallen off sharply. All but one for the last week were from men older than she was—a bad sign. She might well need the posing money to keep her promise to Dena not to touch the savings. She wished she could talk to Dena now.

The first of the fall rains wound in streams down the wall of glass at the back of the studio, and she watched its shadows undulate on her legs, gradually calming her.

*Paint the light,* the art teacher told his students. *Where is the light? What does it want with her? Don't decide. See.*

The rain guttered in the drainpipes outside the windows, stilling and graying the trees and cars outside. A few charcoal pencils etched canvas, then ceased one by one, leaving the room quiet in a way that amplified the rain and the serious smell of paint and oils. Merlinda looked up once, long enough to watch the rivulets snaking the back window so she could remember them after she looked back down at her left foot on the bottom rung of a paint-spattered wooden ladder. She gripped the sides as if she had just descended it. She thought about the streams of rain running down her body, finding riverbeds and floodplains, a hundred small streams wanting to be one. It brought back a Sunday in June at her aunt's when she was a girl, sitting in knee-length cut-offs in the river because her AME aunt wouldn't let her wear a bathing suit. The lines of the current had played in active, watery shadows over her feet and calves. Odis had told Merlinda all storms started in the ocean—the sun sucking seawater into clouds that blew inland until they rained the water out to flow down rivers back to the coast, like the Ocmulgee did to the Atlantic, where the whole cycle repeated itself. Neeta called it foolishness. *Water don't go but one way, child*, she had said. *Can't nobody step in the same river twice.*

After forty-five minutes, she was given a break. She blinked, streams superimposed over the art teacher's face, the paper cup of coffee he brought her, and the students themselves as they milled about, some going in and out the door. She shook her head as if she had a bead of water stuck in one ear.

*You know, you can move your eyes once in a while. No one will die.*

The world cleared.

*I thought you said looking at them makes them uncomfortable.*

*They're painting, Vanessa. Once they get started, they're lost in it.*

*Okay. Got it.*

Merlinda got lost in it, too. She recalled holding still next to Odis on her aunt's back porch, watching a doe graze at the edge of the yard. He had said before anybody white lived in Macon, the Indians had hunted down all the deer for their skins, to trade them for pots, pans, steel knives, and rum. A buckskin was worth a dollar then, he said, which was why people still called a dollar a buck. Merlinda had been horrified—so horrified she hadn't completely believed Odis. She had been pretty gullible then.

By the end of the session her legs and forearms ached. Sitting down brought her a distinct thrill of physical gratitude. As she rested on a metal folding chair, the white robe pulled around her, the teacher had the students turn their easels to face her. She sat confronting three versions of herself, each tightly focused on her form and dissolving into canvas around the edges, as if she were coming out of nothing. An older Puerta Rican girl had given her perfect skin and darkened her eyes to black. Merlinda smiled. She had been brunette seven years ago and hadn't looked like the painting at all.

As the students left, Merlinda stretched her arms over her head, fingers interlocked, popping her back loudly.

*Three paintings I've done, just today*, she said. *It's been a long one.*

The art teacher chuckled and sat down on a bench near her chair. He looked tired. He had been walking around easel to easel for as long as she had stood at the ladder.

*You're joking*, he said, *but this is real work you're doing. It's not easy.*

*Have you done it before?*

*Well. No.* He shrugged, eyebrows up. *Is it easier than your other job?*

*Yes.* She saw his mouth tighten at one corner. *But less satisfying.*

She didn't expect him to look at her but he did. Merlinda laughed, crossing her legs at the knee so that they emerged tanned and aerobic from the split in the robe. The redirection didn't work. He looked her in the face, then away.

*Are we not talking about my marketing work?*

He didn't reply, only watched her—his face not angry but also not readable.

*Come on. I was teasing*, she said. Really, the dates and the posing weren't that different. Get naked and let someone make you into somebody else.

Merlinda had crossed a line. Stupid move on her part. This guy was simple to manage, he was considerate, his appetites were easy. She sighed.

*You get to see what they make you into. That's nice.* She gave him her most plaintive, younger-sister-in-distress smile, remembering the weeks of sorting the responses to the personal ads until she had a base of her kind of clients— married and single professionals and academic types in the right tax bracket, either with a grown man's libido and a fourteen-year-old boy's ego or the other way around. She didn't want to lose him.

*Or maybe you just see what they see, as well as they can show you*, he said.

ॐ

That night he showed up at the carriage house without calling first. Merlinda was there to put a few crime novels on the shelf on the possibility that she might be breaking in a law school professor in the next few days. Not making a date was a big strike against a client—one of the missteps that got a man flagged in Dena's book. *You are not a call girl, Merlie. You are not a convenience.*

But Merlinda was too relieved and grateful she hadn't lost him not to let him in, noticing too late that he had brought a bottle of wine. While working, Merlinda never drank anything she hadn't supplied herself, though naturally she had never said this to a client. She left him in the kitchenette/living room to shuck her minidress and slip into a robe she had bought that matched the one she wore in his classes—a turn-on, she hoped, that would keep him in the rotation. Her mind was already working up a way to avoid the wine.

*You're just what I was hoping for,* she said from the bedroom, then came out with the robe belted exactly as loosely as the real robe was in the art classes.

The art teacher laughed, shaking his head. He drew the pinot noir and a delicate, big-bowled wine glass from a shopping bag with handles, then pulled her corkscrew off the fridge with a click. Before she worked out an escape from the wine in her mind, he was already talking, reacting to the robe.

*That's perfect,* he said. *And I thought it would be a surprise.*

*I thought you might drop in.*

*Well, these are for you, too*, he said, placing the corkscrew alongside the bottle and glass. *Let them be a surprise, even if the canvas isn't. No looking until after I'm gone, okay? Sorry, but I'm weird about that. I know you don't do weird, but this I can't help.*

Just like that he was gone. Merlinda stood there trying to adjust, a little disoriented, unsure what had just happened. The painting was small, fitting freely in the bag. She could see its edge, the mottle of paint there.

After an hour she was sure he wasn't coming back. She went into the bathroom, washed off her carefully composed face, and leaned into the mirror. Her cheeks and chin were grainy as eraser rubbings. Her blonde eyelashes without mascara or liner made her eyes look tiny, the beginnings of crows' feet inching out from the corners.

Halfway through the second glass of wine, she felt fortified enough to look. The painting seemed to bristle and pour. Somehow all her poses were there at once, layered one on top of the other, no one moment covered. Then she saw that the poses deepest down the bubbling well of the canvas weren't poses, but the first episodes between her and the teacher—their meeting at the City Bar, a hint of her leopard print wrap blouse that worked so well—the carriage house door's ornate knob—the schooner from the label of the Pete's Wicked Ale she stocked here for him. His students' sketches and studies of her were there, the best ones, in miniature, each caught in a single gesture. Her alt-faces ascended the ladder, each one higher and clearer until the highest, which was her own, as she had just seen it herself in the mirror, as he had never seen it.

Merlinda never stayed the night at the carriage house if she wasn't working, but that night she did. She couldn't take the painting to Aunt Neeta's. She had a strict rule against having clients' things in her home, and her aunt's house, she realized, was home. Since she didn't want to leave it, her only option was to stay. She took a long bath with a last glass of the pinot, looking through the doorway at the painting propped against the bed, far enough away that it blurred into a tangle of lines and colors and became—what was the word?—abstract. It looked like an oily, rippling puddle. One part rainbow, five parts mess. It looked like her.

ڡ

The art teacher didn't call. Merlinda didn't see him again until Tuesday, the day they would finish her in the oils class. She changed in the same closet she had used the first day, looking again at the eyeball on the back of the door, its window long and curving. She considered digging the eyeliner out of her purse and sprucing it up—maybe adding mascara or scratching *Merlinda was here* in one of the windowpanes. She dropped her bra down her arms and caught it by the strap, folding it cup on cup before she put it in her shoulder bag. The robe felt good in the chilly air. She decided to leave her socks on until the students arrived.

Merlinda opened the door a crack, then stepped out into the empty room. Two kids' canvases were there already, set up on easels. She looked them over, feeling oddly luxurious in the socks and terrycloth, as if she lived there, in a glass-walled gallery, early autumn gingko leaves stuck by rain to her windows. She looked at her unself in the paint, the body stroked into being by the students' young hands. Bryan was painting her with a pallet knife—a narrow, springy, flattened spoon usually used to mix colors. The painting looked harsh and choppy, the pigment smeared and clotted on, but Merlinda liked the idea of being painted with a knife. It suited her.

*Vanessa. Hi.* It was the art teacher.

She glanced over her shoulder at him. *Does it do me justice?*

He laughed in a way she hadn't heard before. *Almost. Bryan's comes a lot closer than the others.*

*I think so, too. It means more when you say it.*

*Why? You have better eyes for yourself than I do.*

*But you're the professional.*

*I think we're both the professional.*

*Whatever you say, teach.*

He smiled, doing that differently too. No teeth.

*I brought your painting back. I really liked it.*

*It's yours. As long as you don't mind if I do more.*

*It's too much. I can't accept it.* But she had already accepted it and she knew it. She saw the wall in Neeta's house where she wanted to hang it, beside the window that looked out on the canebrake and the levee trail.

*Just model an extra class or two.* There was no sign in his face that he expected anything else. She remembered his eyes from that afternoon in her work bed when he had described her. They were different. The problem was that her keeping the portrait meant he couldn't be a client. Gifts, especially romantic ones, screwed up the balance sheet, with clients attaching cash value to them or, worse, emotional property rights.

There was more to this situation than that. Merlinda saw that he really saw her. It was about more than exchange values. He was in deep. She would have to drop him from her book.

The students sifted in, carrying their canvases and tackleboxes. The Puerto Rican woman—Merlinda saw her as a woman now because of the way the other students said *yes ma'am* to her—wore a floppy denim beach hat. There was the familiar bustle of beginning, the sharp scent of paint penetrating the room. The art teacher rubbed his palms together, then clapped them once.

*Okay. Let's finish.*

Merlinda tugged the socks off and poked them into the pocket of the robe before she sloughed it off and dropped it to one side. She stepped onto the ladder's lowest rung. Next session she could leave off the makeup—shock everyone by wearing clothes. Cut-offs.

*Bring her into the world, people.* From the corner of her eye, Merlinda saw him looking at her foot on the ladder, probably imagining it in motion.

*I've been here all along.* As she said it, she decided to stay.

## Going to Water on Wise Creek

Before the canoe carries him, he must first carry the canoe—
from shed to truck, then from Vineville to the river. The
drive requires strong coffee in a cup that won't spill on the
washboard logging roads, music on cassette because that's all
the old truck will play, the rising sun coming sideways into
the cab, and a forbearing foot that lets up on the accelerator
where key slowings, pauses, and silences are called for. He
thinks of his patient foot as a governor—a means of arrest-
ing an engine's speed and power to make arrival more grad-
ual, usually for safety's sake.

The pauses occur on river bridges, where he eyeballs the
water level and looks for snags upstream and down. He has
mastered the timing of rolling down the windows—first the
driver's side, then the passenger's, which requires draping
himself full-length across the cab. They're cranked fully
open exactly at mid-bridge, where he coasts almost to a stop
between Jasper and Butts counties, feeling on his face and
bare arms headwind, tailwind, or calm. It has not occurred
to him how fluidly he leans along the seat to wind down the
glass just before he shifts gears with the same hand, double-
clutching from third gear to second. Gaps in the forest, wild

turkeys, snakes, and high ridges also slow him. Seeing composes a large part of what he has come for.

Once he leaves the state highway—the road steadily roughens the farther from Vineville he goes: pocked asphalt to dirt to gravel to clay—sightings along the road matter as much as they do along the river. These slowings—often at the same places where he has slowed before, so that they have become like stations, making the journey into a ritual— often stretch into pauses. His first drive through, he glimpsed in a clearing of forest two thin puppies he tried to call to him and take home, so that station has become the dog dell. (The same pups in town he would have ignored.) He idles at an overlook on a channel-spanning shoal and sees a slim red creek boat bump over the foaming drop. For ten minutes, he hangs as suspended in his drive by a buzzard's circular glide on a thermal, wings open and still, as the bird is in the sky. Often, there is also salvage of some kind to collect—a length of tie-down strap on the roadside, a tossed cooler good for caught fish, the rusty iron legs off an old sewing machine. These things beg to be returned to use. In spring and early summer, there are turtles he must deliver from the road's middle to its shoulder, planting them in the same direction they pointed when he picked them up so he doesn't stretch their trip. Some cooters close up with a cool hiss as he approaches, deflating their lungs to seal themselves in. He doesn't touch the small, young turtles who might be on their first quest to mate and nest and whose brains are newly mapping the way. The turtles count as pauses and also as silences. Their wholeness and self-

166

containment are profound. What other creature is so perfectly its own home?

The pauses grow more studied and serious as the put-in approaches. Is the creek that crosses the river road too deep to drive through? Will the silt in the lows suck him down to his axels? Will backwater from flood stage end the trip before it begins? He drives always into the threat of logging trucks, of a shiny new padlock on a formerly open chain gate, of a backhoe gouging into the riverside a new house's foundation. These misfortunes are rare, but when they happen they hurt for years. They, too, are silences, but of a different sort—an imposed absence, like when music ceases mid-chord.

The other, better silences speak. The cessation of small talk and sales jingles and the bluster of meetings, the susurrus of Interstate 75 and of elevator music and the televisions that have colonized even schools and churches. In coming to the river, he comes to be entirely subject to a place and to the processes, beauties, and dangers of its persisting, its going on in the oldest worldly way. He is choosing the Ocmulgee's sounds—shoal chuckles, the different sighs of breeze through pine, hickory, and sycamore trees, a rare heron croak, the ratcheting and keening of kingfishers and hawks—which never dominate his senses and which never diminish into the background.

This trip in involves all previous trips in. Today's trip makes a map that is laid over other, earlier trips' maps. The oldest map remains the clearest and most vivid because it was the first, cartographed from failures to arrive. He remembers each of his first three attempts to find this put-in from McElheney's Crossroads: first, a turn that took him toward the river for a mile, then swept him up northerly hills. He had asked for the river and the road gave him a Primitive Baptist church. He returned to McElheney's and asked again, this time to be given gun-blue blackberries and a pole corral holding a mare and dappled foal. Neither was wrong. Neither was the answer he sought. So he accepted both, came again to the crossroads and took the one path left toward the answer he needed. His progress through a suspension of choices and routes illuminated the web of where he was. It felt less like a process of elimination than of exploration—of culmination.

The sight of the river the morning he first found this entry to it will always flash back into his mind when he returns. The deep green of the early summer trees through which he first saw it glitter, the sun scouring the big rocks the water pours around, the foaming gyre below them—all will flow into his awareness, to be re-collected and compared to what he sees now, the river the same story in two different tellings. He will remember the adrenal spurt touched off in his chest by the current's sound—like applause, like an unruly crowd. "And all the trees of the field shall clap their hands," the prophet Isaiah writes—like that, unceasing. The adrenaline doubled at the sight of the water's boil along a bank low enough to launch from.

That sight simultaneously disquiets him and drowns all his excuses. He must go, must commit. Always he comes wanting to meet the river in person and paddle it—but in person her volume and authority take him aback. She is legion, reckless, a downhill riot. She bullies, carves, and butts. A person sees the broken and blasted bed her current has plowed, a hundred casual damages plain in any one rod of riverbank, and the sheath around their soul thins until they can see through it. The best and worst moment in a wild place is the recognition of what one has to lose.

All the choices in getting here have been his. Once he puts his keel to the current he subjects himself to the will of the watershed, saddling himself on the power of all the thunderstorms of summer channeled into one riparian body. He can counter the current, he can resist it, but he can't dominate or outlast it. The important choices are the river's and they can't be unmade. Does he cast his bread upon those waters? Of course he does.

To come through this negotiation with gravity and gush, it is best to be as light as a beaver-stripped stick. The more minimal he makes himself the better. He must not impose. The shape of his boat had better make concessions to the current. His canoe sits lightly on the surface, the face of the flow, where friction with the air makes the water slower than it is below. The curve of bow and keel ease the meeting of the boat and the current. Nose and tail never directly oppose the river's will with edges or hard lines. Rounded front, bottom, and back, the canoe could be coming or going. The vessel conducts flow, meets and manages it, alternating between acquiescence and deflection in a conversation that can be felt through the gunwales and stern. In the river's argument with itself, his canoe must not take a side—must find and ride the middle, that line of tension. He tunes to it. He feels it like a harmonic where the boat seat cradles his rear. He remembers the buzzard on the thermal, wings still as a sail, accepting the ride.

At dusk, when he rounds the bend below the last islet of rock and sees the bridge like a worn, ordinary altar, like a gate through which he must not pass, he won't know how to figure how long he has been borne along. River miles and hours accrue by their own weird math. The Ocmulgee's additions, subtractions, and divisions are geological, alluvial, animal, arboreal. Together, they make one whole alluviation—a fluid progression of a thousand contrary forces. This largest flow can't be seen at human scale, but he senses it in the way both time and its measurement dissolved once he entered this current. Every river hour that passes leaves a remainder of infinity. How many springs will the last above-water branch of the submerged sycamore that toppled four years ago bud out into broad green leaves? The pebbles below Smith Shoals are perfected and yet their polishing purls on. The forms of the constant white breakers below Big Sneak remain while the changing flow of their substance goes and goes. All the river is both particle and wave.

By the time his prow creases the silt at the bottom of the take-out ramp with a gritty kiss, there isn't much he knows. To wash away what he does, he takes a seat in the clear, sandy shallows. Soon his friend will be here in his pickup and they will carry to it the canoe that has carried him, then go. For now, he sits in the current, his body a flag rippling in the Ocmulgee's steady blow.

# Notes

The Ocmulgee River's name may derive from the Hitchiti words *oki* (water) and *molki (bubbling* or *boiling)*, together meaning "where the water bubbles up." There are strong associations between the Native people and the river that sustained them and that was so central to their culture; English traders from the Carolinas called these people living along the Fall Line the *Oka-mole-ke* ("water swirling people") or "Okmulgees." These indigenous people living along its banks above the Fall Line knew the river as *Ochese-hatchee* as late as the early 1800s, when the stream marked the western border of the United States. The culture that developed along the river continues today in the Muscogee Nation, a self-governing union of tribes that makes its home in Okmulgee, Oklahoma, though the Ocmulgee Old Fields remain sacred to them.

In "The Only Place to Start From," John Mark's simple understanding of Mississippian and Muscogee cultural practices is based on his reading of Charles Hudson's *The Southeastern Indians*, Bartram's *Travels*, Walter Harris's *Here the Creeks Sat Down*, and other illustrated books the boy has "borrowed" from the bookstore at Ocmulgee

Mounds National Historical Park, and on displays from the park's Visitors Center museum.

The baptism and burying ground in "Burying Ground" are based on sacred practices in the African-American tradition in the South described in Annie Staten and Susan Roach's "Take Me to the Water: African-American River Baptism." While baptisms have been conducted on the Ocmulgee and its tributaries, the story's baptismal ground on the east bank of the river at Juliette is a fiction.

Odis's readings about the upper Ocmulgee in "Seven Islands" include the books mentioned in the note about John Mark above as well as Hudson's *Knights of Spain, Warriors of the Sun*, Hudson's *Ocmulgee Archaeology, 1936-1986*, David Corkran's *The Creek Frontier*, James Mooney's *History, Myths, and Sacred Formulas of the Cherokee*, and narratives of the de Soto Expedition composed by Rodrigo Ranjel and by the anonymous "gentleman of Elvas." Odis was also an avid collector of oral histories of the river.

In "A Ferry and Four Keeper Holes," a keeper hole (also known as a souse hole or a hydraulic) is a strong circular current, usually found below a drop, that captures anything washed into it and recirculates it again and again from the surface of the river to the bottom. In the early 1800s, when the Ocmulgee was the western boundary of the United States, the east bank was commonly known as "white side" and the west as "Ind'in" or "Injun side."

# About the Author

Gordon Johnston is the author of *Scaring the Bears* (Mercer, 2021) and has written two chapbooks, *Durable Goods* (Finishing Line Press) and *Gravity's Light Grip* (Perkolator Press), co-authored a guide to *Ocmulgee Mounds National Historical Park*, and published poems and prose in The *Georgia Review, Southern Poetry Review*, and other journals. He also writes clay pages—poems wood-fired into stoneware by Roger Jamison. Director of the Georgia Poetry Circuit from 1996–2007, Johnston is professor of English at Mercer University.